Fallen Rayne

Five Sloths Brewing Book 1

Robin Andrews

Fallen Rayne
Five Sloths Brewing, Book 1
Robin Andrews

Published by STE Entertainment LLC

Copyright 2020 STE Entertainment LLC
Edited by Holly Funk
ISBN: 978-1-7345279-0-2

Five Sloths Brewing logo and cover art designed by Dee J Holmes, Bad
Unicorn Design

Dedication

I dedicate this book, my first book, to so many authors that have inspired me over the last several years. The ones that gave me worlds to read about and heroes to love. Lexi Blake, Shayla Black, Jenna Jacob, Laurelin Paige, Ruth Cardello, and Cherise Sinclair, to name a few.

But, most of all, I thank the woman who sat with me at a book convention and over a glass of wine (or two) helped me find my way to starting this whole process of my "brand." Sierra Cartwright, I can never thank you enough for sitting there and hitting me with the "hard" questions that made me have to figure out who I was and what I write.

This book also would have never gotten written without gentle (and sometimes not so gentle) nudges and advice from friends and family, most especially my husband, who often had to run real life (like letting the dog out) so that I could focus on getting this stuff that has been rattling around in my head down on paper.

I have a whole list of people that I would thank, but the dedication would take forever, and there are more books coming, so I will thank them another time.

Prologue

Rayne felt the heat of the stage lights, the eyes of the crowd, and the excitement of the other dancers and coaches watching backstage as she walked out to the mark that only she could see, her starting point for the performance of a lifetime. If she could pull this off, if she could do this one dance perfectly, flawlessly, she would be in. She would be asked to join the finest ballet troupe in the country. Since she was four, she had dreamed of this, she had practiced endlessly, she had followed every strenuous diet and exercise routine her coaches had expected of her. She had loved dance for as long as she could remember, all kinds of dance really, but her forte, the one her hopes and dreams were built on, was ballet.

The music started and she went through the steps she knew probably as well as she knew how to walk. The moves had become a second nature to her; the fluid movements of her body were things that came almost as natural to her as breathing.

When the music ended, she took her bow, trying to not jump up and down and squeal with delight. Instead, she looked toward the ceiling and quietly said, "That was for you, Daddy. This one was for you." She knew in her heart she had nailed it. Every pirouette had been perfect, all her cabriole had landed exactly as they were supposed to, her extensions fluid. It had been as perfect as she could possibly dance. She was certain that she would win the audition, she would be with the New York Ballet soon. Her dreams were all about to come true.

Chapter One

Three months later

Walt cleared his throat to get the attention of the young woman who was sitting staring out the window. Apparently, she hadn't heard his knock on the door, so he had pushed it open slightly to see if anyone was inside. She appeared to be lost in thought. When she heard him, she turned toward him, and he realized he was looking at the single most beautiful woman he had ever seen. Her skin was pale olive, her hair was a long wavy auburn mass that flowed most of the way down her back, her cheekbones were high and perfect, but her eyes, although a beautiful rich amber, were haunted, almost like there was no life in them. It took him aback for a moment to see someone so beautiful yet so lifeless inside.

He cleared his throat again to try to regain some control of the voices inside his head, the voices telling him that this woman needed him, and as more than just an attorney. He suddenly wanted to help her find life again. He just wasn't sure how to do that. He stepped into the room, reaching out his hand to her as he drew closer. "Hello, Ms. Davis. I'm Walter Jensen, your attorney." She took his hand, but again, he almost felt like there was no life in the woman sitting in front of him. Yes, obviously, she was alive, she was breathing, and she spoke softly when she said, "Hello." But there was no life there, not really, no vibrancy that he would expect from a woman so young and so beautiful. "I'm here to ask you a few questions so that we can get started on your case, if that's all right with you."

"That's fine," she said. "The sooner we get this taken care of, the sooner those bastards pay for what they did to me."

Ah, there was the life, at least a small spark of it, although not in the way he wanted to see her eyes light with emotion. This was pure loathing, utter hatred for the persons involved in the lawsuit he was hopefully going to win for her. Maybe that would give her some happiness. He very likely could make her a very rich woman with this case. After all, the defendant was obviously negligent. For some reason, though, he got the sense that money wasn't really going to do anything to change her demeanor. He also got the sense that those eyes would be almost like a slow burning flame if she were truly passionate about something. If she were truly passionate about someone. He briefly pictured those eyes staring into his with a different type of passion.

Whoa!! Walt, what the hell, dude? Totally not appropriate to be drooling over the client. Even if she was the most beautiful woman he had ever seen. He had seen his share of women and had probably dated more than his share. Being an attorney, a part owner of a microbrewery and a former frat boy at a prestigious law school, he had always seen beautiful women and truth be told, he had taken several of them to bed. But there was something about this woman. Maybe it was her sadness, maybe it was her physical beauty, and maybe it was the fact that she was a victim of a horrible injustice, but whatever it was, he was reacting to her like he had never reacted to someone before.

Get your head back in the game, Walt, he silently scolded himself. Yeah, it would seem totally professional to be drooling like a school kid for the initial interview with a new client. The thing was, though, that even though his body had definite thoughts about her, there was something else too. It wasn't a sexual draw, not that he would say there was nothing sexual to this, but there was something about this woman that made him want to put a smile back on her face, to see her lively and vibrant again. He had no doubt that at one point she had been vivacious and happy. Her case file said she had been a dancer all her life, so she had obviously had a deep passion for something—well, something other than revenge, that is.

He hesitated, not quite sure how to move forward. He had seen plaintiffs before that were bitter, he had seen ones that were in pain, he had seen ones that were angry, but he honestly didn't remember ever seeing one that seemed like the incident had literally taken the life from her. Finally, he shook his head to get his mind back on the matter at hand.

"Yes, well, of course," he said, trying to figure out how to move forward with the questions he needed to ask her. "First of all, thank you for taking the time to talk to me today. I think we have a great chance of winning this case. I believe it's pretty cut and dried that the construction company was negligent. I am very optimistic that we will get a very generous settlement."

"How much can they possibly pay? There is no amount that will get my life back. Life is over for me; no amount of money can fix that. But yes, I do want to make them pay, I want to make them pay to the point that they have to go out of business, I want to ruin their lives as much as they have ruined mine." The words came out almost like venom; there was pure hatred behind them. He had been wrong, it wasn't that there wasn't any life there; it was just that the life that was there was so bitter and hateful that she couldn't focus on anything but making someone pay for the situation she found herself in.

"Yes, well." Again, he found himself not knowing exactly how to respond. This petite beautiful woman was so hateful, so spiteful, so....so.... and that was when he saw what she really was. She was so hurt, so horribly, completely broken that she did not know how to even function in a normal manner. Maybe his best bet would be to try to find out from others what they felt had happened to her. Not the details of the accident, he could read those in the reports, but what had really happened to her, to the lively young woman that he could tell had been in there at some point.

"Actually, maybe it would be best if I get you to sign some release forms for me so that I can talk to your doctors and the other medical staff involved in your case, I might be able to get a better idea of what we are dealing with from them, before you and I sit and talk strategy for the case."

"That's fine. Whatever you need from me. I just want to get this over with," she said softly.

He gave her the usual forms, the retainer naming him as her attorney in the case of Rayne Davis vs Charmichael Construction, releases of her medical files, permission to talk with doctors, therapists, police, and anyone else who might have any insight into her case.

She signed paper after paper, pretty much before he had a chance to explain to her what she was signing.

"Are you sure you don't want to read over any of these before you sign them?" he asked.

She looked up at him and again, he was touched deeply by the lifelessness of her eyes. "I'm sure that there is nothing in here that can harm me any more that what this incident has already done. If you are worried that I may be signing away things that I shouldn't, trust me, Mr. Jensen, I don't believe I have anything more to lose than my life and the future I dreamed of."

Walt walked out of the room at the rehabilitation facility almost in a fog. He felt something so deeply for that young woman. It wasn't pity, not really. Although he did feel extreme sorrow, it wasn't pity, it was a deep and utter sickening at the pain and loss that he had seen in that young woman's face. He vowed that he would do whatever it took to bring life back to those eyes. He knew it wasn't about money for her, so he had to figure out what it was about. And then he needed to fix whatever it was. He wouldn't stop, he wouldn't rest until he saw some spark of life in her eyes again. He just wasn't sure how he was going to do that.

****

Rayne sadly shook her head as the attorney left her room. That was one handsome man. She had never really had much experience with men. She had always been so involved in her dancing, from lessons to exercise to choreography planning, that she had never really had time for boys when she was younger and definitely not for men once she got old enough to start working toward becoming a member of the New York City Ballet. She had always thought there would be time for that later. Most prima ballerinas didn't work much past the age of thirty or thirty-five. She was only twenty-three. She'd thought she had plenty of time for dating and marriage and children, later, after her career had peaked. Now, though, she would never know that life. Who would want to marry a woman who was so sad, so utterly broken that she didn't see the way to ever be happy again? Life was just throwing her all kinds of hard hits lately. She'd lost her dream to dance and then she lost her dream to have a family someday.

No, she knew that she would always be alone. No one would find her attractive, no one would want to be involved with someone like her. A woman that was possibly never going to get out of a wheelchair or at best would have a horrible limp. But still, she couldn't help but think about how gorgeous that man had been, with his deep black hair and those emerald green eyes. Well, at least she would have a good-looking man around long enough for her lawsuit to finish. Even if there was no hope of having someone like him in her life forever.

Chapter Two

Walt made his first stop at the office of the doctor that was currently in charge of Rayne's case. Dr. Worthington was an older man, probably early 60s. He had the typical "doctor" look, as Walt liked to say. Hair that was graying around the temples, although not enough to make him look anything beyond "distinguished" and not at all "old." Glasses that sat just slightly too low on his nose, like possibly he only really used them for reading. Generic looking pants, tie and dress shirt beneath his traditional white lab coat. Nothing that one wouldn't expect from a surgeon of his age and apparent skill.

He was escorted into the doctor's office by the receptionist. "Hello, Doctor Worthington. I'm Walter Jensen," he said, reaching over the desk to shake hands with the older gentleman. "I'm representing Rayne Davis in her lawsuit for her recent injury. I'd like to ask you a few questions if I may."

"Of course," the doctor replied, shaking Walt's hand. "I'll do anything I can to help get that young woman on her way to healing."

"What do you mean? Does she need more surgery? Are there injuries that are still causing issues for her?" Walt asked. Maybe that had been why he had seen such pain in her eyes. Maybe she really was in physical pain and it just showed on her face. He had thought that she was done with any medical treatment other than the rehabilitation aspect to try to get her stronger and regain more muscle tissue and range of motion.

"No, no," he said, slightly shaking his head. "I've done all I can medically. As far as her x-rays and tests, she is healed as much as she can be. Of course, she needs the physical therapy for a few more weeks. But that is mostly to help her adjust to her situation and for her muscles to build back up after an injury and having to be immobile for an extended period. No, that girl needs to heal in ways that have nothing to do with my skill as a doctor." He shook his head sadly.

"So physically, she is done with surgery and anything else other than the PT. She is almost back to normal?" Walt asked.

"Normal? Well, not back to what she was before the accident, no." He was struggling with his words, almost as if he didn't know exactly how to say what he wanted to say. Walt wasn't sure if he was struggling with what he could share as her doctor or if it was something else. It appeared he was speaking more as a friend, or someone who at least cared about her, maybe admired her in some way. "Physically, I have done all I can for her. Her bones are healed. Her nerves suffered some damage, but not so much that she is still paralyzed. She has had some loss of physical ability, but she is by no means a paraplegic; she doesn't need to stay in that wheelchair. The problem is that she has to want to do her therapy. She has to want to work to get back as much as she can." He looked sad as he added, "She will never dance professionally again, but there is absolutely no reason she can't walk and lead a normal life. She could even dance, for enjoyment but most likely not professionally. She will most likely always have a slight limp. The true problem lies in her brain. She has given up and if she doesn't begin being proactive in her therapy and healing process, her muscles will continue to atrophy. If that happens, the likelihood of being able to walk becomes less and less the longer she doesn't participate in therapy."

Walt took a moment to process what the doctor had told him. She could be better, she could walk again, but she had to want to. How was he supposed to help her want to? What could he do to give her a reason to want to live—not just breathe and have a heartbeat, but live, a life outside of this place, a life outside of that chair? Could he find the key to helping her find life again? He wasn't sure why he felt the need to do so, but he did. There was no way that he could stand by and watch a beautiful young woman who should be full of life sit back and not live anymore.

He looked at the doctor, sure that the desperation was plain on his face, and asked, "Why won't she participate in therapy? Does she have a reason? Does she say why she won't try to progress as far as she can? Does she feel the pain is still too great?"

The doctor shook his head. "All I know is that she seems to have given up. I know she was a dancer; I honestly don't know why she is so against therapy. You would probably get better answers to that from the therapist assigned to her case."

Walt stood to take his leave. "Thank you, Doctor. If I have any other questions, I will be sure to contact you."

Doctor Worthington paused for a moment before looking up at Walt with a sad smile on his face. "I hope you can find a way to help her, young man. I really do."

So apparently Walt wasn't the only one that sensed that his young client needed to find something to make her want to do therapy. He wasn't the only one that wanted to see life in her eyes again. She had that effect on people. No one could see something that was so beautiful and not want to see her reach her full potential.

He made his way down the halls to the physical therapy area of the center and asked to speak to Rayne's therapist. After Walt showed the receptionist the proper documentation that he had a right to be there and that he had Rayne's permission to talk to staff, the receptionist pointed him toward a young woman in scrub pants and a T-shirt. She had her hair pulled back into a ponytail and Walt thought she didn't look like she could have been much more than 20. It bothered him that his brain would go there, but maybe the problem was that Rayne needed someone with a little more knowledge and experience. Maybe this girl was just too young to really understand how to motivate a more "difficult" case. After he talked to her, if he felt anything other than total professionalism and the ability to motivate her clients, he might talk to Rayne's doctor again to see if a change in therapists was in order.

Well, here goes nothing, he thought to himself as he walked over to the young woman.

She looked up from the file she was writing in as Walt approached. "Can I help you?" she asked.

Yep, he had been right; she couldn't have been more than 20, young, most likely naïve about cases where the client maybe needed more motivation than the typical.

"Yes, I hope you can," he replied. He pulled a business card from his pocket and handed it to her. "I'm Walt Jensen, the attorney representing Rayne Davis. I would like to ask you a few questions about her case. I have a signed release here." He showed the paper to the woman, who read it thoroughly before handing it back to him. He got the feeling that she wasn't really happy to have to talk to him about this. Most likely because she knew she was the one lacking when it came to Rayne's care.

"What would you like to know, Mr. Jensen?" She seemed like she was talking to him grudgingly, not willing to openly share any more information than was necessary.

"Well, I would like to start with the extent of her injuries. Her doctor filled me in on the medical aspects for the most part, but I would like to know what you are hoping to accomplish with therapy. How much function can she expect to regain? What is her prognosis, in your opinion?" He was firing the questions at her rapidly, hoping to throw her off balance, and maybe see how she handled pressure. Partially because she might have to testify at the hearing and partially because he really did want to try to determine just how good she was as a therapist for a woman who had lost so much.

She didn't seem to mind his overbearing manor. She just stood up and looked him in the eye and said, "Well, I can't tell you much more about her injuries than her doctor most likely already has. He is the expert in that area, of course. I can, however, tell you about her therapy and just exactly what she is costing herself by not actively participating in her sessions."

So the little therapist had some backbone to her. "Okay, then tell me what you know," he said.

Open and leading questions were always best. Let the person show you how much or how little they really know about the topic. Many an "expert" witness had hung themselves because of that very tactic. If you didn't know your stuff, it was easy to answer yes or no or some other fluff that sounded good but had no real basis in fact. If they did know their job, they could easily give you an entire dissertation on the topic. He waited to see if she flinched at his attitude. She didn't, so she was either good at talking about her job, or she was good at blowing smoke up someone's ass. One thing was for certain: she wouldn't be doing that to him without him calling her on it. This case was too important. He didn't even want to ask himself what it was about this case that made it feel like the most important one he had worked in his entire life.

"Well, clinically, she has some muscle and nerve damage that will never be fully back to what it was before; however, she could improve from where she is now greatly, with therapy and the will to do so." She sounded like she was almost giving a report in front of her professors.

He was starting to get angry. How could this woman act so nonchalant about a client who was basically dying inside because of her loss? "You haven't told me anything that the doctor didn't say. I need to know if you are the person that can help her. I need to know if you will be able to stand up in court and not only tell her injuries but also how hard she has to work to get back to some semblance of life." He knew he was raising his voice, but for some reason he couldn't seem to help it at this point.

Her eyes began to squint, and her nostrils flared just a little. So maybe he wasn't the only one that was angry about this. "Look, Mr. Jensen. Rayne is not a client to me, at least, not just any client. She is only a few years younger than me. I attended the same ballet school as she did for years. I can remember even as a little girl watching her dance. My God, she was beautiful. Every step flowed, her face told you that she was absolutely in love with the dance. Her body was so in tune with the music that her dance absolutely flowed. All of us girls in her classes used to watch her win competition after competition and we could only hope that we could come close to being as good as she was someday. She was the one who had 'IT'; she was the one who could have been the best of the best." She paused to breathe; the entire tirade had seemingly been uttered on a single breath. "You have no idea how much I wished I could be her someday. And you have no idea how much it kills me to see her come in here day after day, not willing to try. She will allow me to attach her to machines that do the work for her, she will allow massage and things meant to help relieve strain and pain. But she will not put any physical effort into getting better. I cannot force her to do the exercises, Mr. Jensen, but it kills me inside to know that she has given up." She got right up in his face and that was no easy thing for a woman that had to be close to a foot shorter than him. She even poked him in the chest with her finger. "So, Mr. Jensen, don't think that I don't give everything I have to try to help her get better, but she has to want it for herself. Nothing I learned in school can make her better if she won't try, but don't you dare imply that I am not doing my absolute best to get her to."

So the therapist was more of a spitfire than he had imagined. Maybe he had been wrong; she really did seem to care about his client. He had to take a few minutes to try to figure out where to go from here. Finally, he asked, "What do you mean? What 'it' did she have? How can I understand just exactly what all she has lost and what all she has gone through?" He really did want to know.

"Talk to her dance coach, talk to the people at the studio, hell, look for newspaper articles," she said with frustration. "She was on her way to the New York City Ballet, she was destined to be one of the best ballerinas in the country, maybe even the world. Look, I get that to you this is just another case, just another settlement to win, but if you can't care about the person, let someone else take her case. She needs someone who cares about more than the dollar signs." She gave him a look that was intimidating for a girl who couldn't be more than 5'2" and maybe a hundred pounds soaking wet.

He was taken aback for a moment. Maybe this therapist did care more than he had given her credit for. The question on her face was one that he wasn't sure how to answer yet. Did he care? Was this more than another case to win for him? The odd part was that for the first time in his legal career, he kind of thought that he did care, far more than a normal attorney-client relationship.

An hour later, Walt sat outside the dance studio, trying to sort things out in his head. What was it about this case that was hitting him so differently? Was it because the client was beautiful? Not likely; he had not only seen but often dated beautiful women. It couldn't simply be because she was beautiful. It was most likely the haunted look in her eyes. Walt didn't remember ever seeing anyone who looked so young and vibrant on the outside but seemed so dead on the inside. More than any other case he had ever had, he needed to understand exactly what she had lost. He felt a deep need to somehow fix this for her. It wasn't about the money, he knew that; the money never really fixed anything. Although, in some cases, it could go a long way to helping to improve the quality of life of some clients, this wouldn't be one of those situations. He knew in his gut that this woman needed something more than the simple monetary reward that he would go after in court. Well, he thought, no time like the present to try to figure out just what this case was truly all about. He got out of his car and started for the studio.

An hour later, Walt was beginning to get a much clearer picture of just what it was that his client had lost. He had seen pictures of her with medals and trophies; he had seen videos of her dancing. There was no doubt about it: she was beautiful in those moments when she seemed totally immersed in the music and her dance. The coach had explained to him what being asked to join the New York City Ballet had meant to her. It wasn't monetary, it wasn't the prestige, it was the feeling of finally making it. It had been a dream come true, and before she had even gotten to perform with them one time, she'd had a horrific accident and would very likely never dance like that again. That was what caused that look in her eyes. She'd literally lost her life that day. Oh, not the walking and talking, the breathing and the beating of her heart. That could go on for years to come, but without the thing that she loved most in life, she would be a shell of her former self. She wouldn't likely smile like he had seen in so many pictures and videos that day. She would continue to be the shell of a woman he had seen sitting in the wheelchair, staring blankly out the window of the rehab facility.

That was another thing that he had noticed: her room. It was bland and bare, as though still in the sterile state an empty room would be. He had seen other patients' rooms as he had walked down the hall. Many had added personal touches. He had seen through open doors bright curtains, pillows or stuffed animals on the beds. Some had pictures on walls and covering every surface in the room. It was a short- to long-term facility. Some patients were only there for a few weeks; others would be there for much longer periods. Some had lost limbs and were learning how to function in a totally different world than they had ever known before. If he had to be in a facility like that, he believed that he would want to make it as much of a home as he possibly could. But Rayne hadn't done that. Her room was still the sterile white and beige that all rooms started out as. There was no color, no personal touches. It was like she just didn't really care anymore at all what her world looked like.

"Excuse me," Walt said to the coach, who had sat him in front of the video monitor twenty minutes earlier. "I have a couple more questions, if I may."

"Sure, anything at all," the older woman said. "I would do anything to help that girl. She has always been someone I care very deeply for, and not just because she was a great dancer with unlimited potential."

Walt could sense a bit of an accent coming through, maybe Russian, or something similar. It wasn't a strong thing, but when she got emotional, as she had a few times when talking about Rayne, you could hear the slight change.

"First, is there anything that you can think of that would help her?"

"Honestly, that is something I ask myself every day," the woman stated sadly. "She has revolved around dance for so long that I don't know what else there is in her life. Her parents are both gone. Her mother has been gone for years, and her father passed a few years ago. She has always been very active in dance, but when her father died, it seemed like she threw herself into it even more. I suppose that's to be expected when someone has no family." She seemed to be thinking of something, her mind far away for a few moments. But she shook her head as if trying to clear a fog and looked back at Walt, waiting for his next question. "I can remember her father bringing her here for classes. He was always there, every recital, every competition. Rayne used to tell me that her daddy had been her first dance partner. When she was little, he would spin her around the kitchen and dance with her. She always said she fell in love with dancing because of him."

That revelation also hurt Walt. So was she alone in the world. No parents, no family–did she have anyone? Walt needed to know. "Did she have siblings, close friends? She wasn't completely alone in the world, was she?"

"No siblings, but she does have a very close friend. A young woman named Sunni. I don't remember her last name; she took lessons here briefly. I suppose trying to have something in common with her friend. She wasn't much of a dancer, at least not ballet. But she was close to Rayne. I could try to find the old records to see if I can find a last name, but if my guess is correct, she most likely visits Rayne regularly. You would most likely be able to find out more about her from the rehabilitation facility than you could from me."

Walt thanked the woman for her information and began walking toward the door. "Young man," the woman called to him just before he got to it. "I know that this doesn't sound possible at the moment, with the way Rayne feels right now, but I truly believe that dance is the answer to helping her find her way back to herself." Walt started to open his mouth to protest, but the woman held up her hand and continued, "Oh, I know, she will never dance like she did before, I am not saying to try to encourage her to try to become a prima ballerina again, but somehow, dance is what I believe will bring the life back to Rayne's eyes. If you truly care about her, find a way to do that."

Now Walt was more confused than ever. How was he supposed to get a woman who refused to participate in her own therapy to even consider trying to dance again?

Chapter Three

Two days later, Walt found himself sitting in the lobby area of the rehab facility. A phone call to Rayne's therapist had given him all the information he had needed about the friend that Mrs. Boullard had told him about. Rayne did indeed have a friend named Sunni who visited her regularly. Her weekday visits were unpredictable; most likely she stopped by when she had the time during the week. But Saturday mornings were like clockwork for the young woman. She was there at 9 a.m. every Saturday and spent a good portion of the day with Rayne. The therapist had described the woman to him so he would know who he was looking for. Basically, her name fit her looks. If you could find a woman who epitomized the name Sunni, you probably had the right woman. A beautiful woman with long straight blond hair walked in. That had to be her. The sunshine literally personified. Walt stood and called out "Excuse me, Sunni?"

The woman turned to see who had called her name. She scowled briefly before saying, "Um, do I know you?"

"No, you don't. I'm Walt, Walt Jensen. I'm the attorney representing Rayne Davis in her lawsuit against the construction company," he said, holding out his business card.

She took the card from him and looked him in the eye, saying, "Good. I hope you make those bastards pay. Although no amount of money will truly ever help her heal, they still need to pay."

So it seemed that everyone agreed on the two most important points. One, the construction company and their employees who had been negligent needed to pay, more as a punishment than anything. And it seemed everyone agreed that no amount of money in the world was going to help Rayne want to come back to life.

"Listen," he began, running his fingers through his hair. "I have met Rayne, I've talked to her doctor, her therapist and her dance coach. No one seems to have a clue how to really help her. I agree with you, no amount of money is going to do it. But I have no clue what will. I was wondering if we could possibly set up a time to talk. I'd like to get your input on how best to help Rayne."

She hesitated at first. He wasn't sure if it was his approach or the subject matter itself that had her seeming to not want to talk to him. But he had to try again; he had to find a way to help Rayne. "Look, I know you are here to visit her, I don't want to hold you up any longer, but it really would help me understand the case better if we could just sit down for a half hour or so. If you want to make sure that is okay with Rayne before we talk, I totally understand." He needed to convince this woman to help him; she was the only one that he felt had the ability to do so. "Okay, well, let's leave it at this then," he said. "I am part owner of Five Sloths Brewing." She looked at him with an amused look on her face. "I know, odd name for a brewery, it's kind of a long story. Anyway, I'll be there all evening. I would really appreciate it if you would stop by and talk to me, even for a few minutes. I'll buy the beer," he added, kind of jokingly, kind of not. Whatever it took to get this woman to agree to talk to him was well worth it. "Hey, I'll even throw in the story of how we came up with the name of the brewery. What have you got to lose?" Then he realized that there was one more thing that just might convince her to show up. "I understand your hesitance to talk about your friend, but all I can tell you is the first time I walked into that room, I saw the most beautiful woman I've ever seen with the most haunted almost dead eyes I've ever looked into. If there is anything that I can do to change that look, I have to try." He knew he sounded sort of desperate to talk to this woman, and maybe he was, but something had to work.

Sunni hesitated a few more moments before looking up into his eyes. She seemed to be analyzing him. Then she finally said "Okay, you seem genuine about this. I'll give you a half hour. Tonight at 7. If Rayne is okay with it, that is." She turned to walk to her friend's room. Just as he was starting to turn and walk toward his car, Sunni turned and added, "Oh, and Mr. Jensen, I definitely want to hear the sloth story." He saw the smile briefly cross her face before she turned again and headed down the hall.

Finally, maybe some answers. He was going to do his best to convince Sunni to not only answer his questions but also help him figure out how to help Rayne.

Chapter Four

Walt was at the brewery at five that evening. He was nervous about this meeting for some reason. Maybe because a part of him almost felt like a beautiful young life depended on the outcome of this discussion. One of his co-owners Jason was there too. They all took turns managing for the evening, although after the five years they had been working on building and staffing the pub/brewery, they really did have a staff that could run the place without the help of any of the owners. Really, it was more about the fact that they all liked to meet their customers, they liked to talk and get input from the people who dined and drank at their establishment. It never hurt to have one of the owners on hand to respond if there were a complaint or a compliment to be heard.

"Hey," Jason said when he caught sight of Walt. "Did you forget tonight wasn't your night to manage, or did you think I can't handle the crowd?" He had a big smile on his face, and Walt knew he was just yanking his chain.

"Nah, man," Walt responded. "I'm meeting someone here for the case I'm working on. It just seemed like she wasn't willing to open up and talk much, so I thought maybe the atmosphere here would be more relaxing. I'm going to set up at our table. She's not due till around seven, so I'm going to go over some case notes." The table he referred to was one that was sort of set off by itself. It was still very much in the public part of the pub, but the layout of the place had lent itself to an area that was in a sort of alcove of windows. It was a table that for the most part wasn't ever given to a regular patron; that way the guys could use it if they had a date or if they just needed some privacy to be able to talk freely. Kind of like he felt he did tonight.

"Oh, yeah," he said, turning back toward Jason. "Her name is Sunni and as it was explained to me, when you see a woman walk in who looks like a Sunni, that's probably her."

Jason smiled and replied, "Ah, well, if she is at all how she sounds, I may just have to distract her for a while before I point her in your direction."

Walt started laughing and shaking his head. "Look, manwhore," he said quietly. "It really is about a case, and it really is important to me. Don't go molesting my informants so they want to leave before I get the information I need."

Jason laughed along with Walt, "Okay, okay, I'll wait until after you get your info before I try to seduce her."

It was ten minutes to seven when Walt heard a soft feminine voice say, "Mr. Jensen?" He hadn't realized the time had passed so quickly. He had been so immersed in his current case his mind had been racing trying to think of how to win it. Oh, not win it monetarily; he was pretty sure that was a done deal. After all, the company had been negligent, that wouldn't be hard to prove. In fact, he wouldn't be surprised if the company's attorney contacted him at some point with an offer. He was more concerned about how to win the far more personal aspect of giving a young woman the will to want to live her life to its fullest extent.

He stood to pull out a chair so Sunni could sit down and said, "Please, call me Walt. Mr. Jensen makes me think my father is here, and besides, I am hoping that this won't be completely a business meeting." She looked at him like she was about ready to get back up and leave. He had offended her; she had thought he was hitting on her. "No, wait, let me rephrase that. I hope that we can find a way to work together to help Rayne. I don't want to just get her a large financial settlement; I am hoping to figure out a way to make her want to live a life outside of a wheelchair in a rehab facility. I am hoping you can help me with that."

She settled into her chair more comfortably. Apparently his explanation had made her feel more at ease. As he rounded the table to retake his seat, he noticed Jason behind the bar. His friend gave him a double thumbs-up with a big smile as he took in the woman sitting there. *Yep, manwhore extraordinaire*, he thought. Oh well, it wasn't his place to tell Jason how to live his life, if he didn't ruin the rapport Walt was trying to build with his client's bestie.

"So," Walt began. "I have lots of questions for you and any input you have will be highly appreciated."

Sunni shook her head with a look of mischief in her eyes. "No, counselor, sloth story first, then we'll see how willing I am to answer your questions." Walt could tell she wasn't totally serious. She really did want to help her best friend, but she wasn't going to just roll over and give up all her intel.

He groaned a little but then started the story of how Five Sloths Brewing came to be. "Well, the idea sort of started with me and four of my frat brothers. We all went to college together, joined the same frat, and we all knew we were headed for the same law school. We were all ambitious in our pursuit of education. We were always at the top of our classes, usually competing for the best grades and the titles like Summa Cum Laude or whatever." He didn't want to make it sound like bragging; it really wasn't. Yes, they had all done well in school, but it wasn't about showing off, it was about the fact that they had all grown up sons of very high achieving families. Three of them had fathers who owned one of the largest law firms in Grand Rapids, Michigan. Of the other two, one's dad was a state supreme court justice, and the other was the son of a senator. Pretty much political science ran in their blood. "Anyway," he continued, "we were frat boys, so of course, we loved beer. We started tossing around the idea of opening our own brewery when we passed the bar. No pun intended," he said with a smile. "Fast forward a few years and we were all out of school, some working for my dad and some for the other dad's law firm. It was time to make our plan happen. We started building this place, researched who the best micro brewers were, and the dream started to take shape, so to speak. The problem was, we needed a name. I believe it was one night after we had probably sampled way too many brews from the brewers we were considering hiring when we were all sitting around trying to come up with a name. Someone suggested that with all the years that we had spent working our asses off to get the grades and to pass the bar, the ironic thing would be to call ourselves the five sloths. Sort of an oxymoron to what our lives had been up to that point." He could tell she was sort of trying to hold back a chuckle, and who wouldn't when presented with that story? It wasn't an overly appealing name in a lot of ways, but their business was becoming a success, silly name or not. "So, did my story warrant some answers from you?" he asked, hopeful.

"The story, while rather funny, isn't why I am here or why I will help you in any way I can," she admitted. "For some reason, I think that what you said earlier is really true. You do want to help Rayne, and it's not about the money. For whatever reason, you want to help her." She corrected herself, "Actually, no, I won't say 'for whatever reason.' I know the reason; Rayne is a very special woman. Even though she isn't herself right now, you obviously saw what those of us who love her already know. Under all her hurt and pain, she has a beautiful soul."

"You're right," he agreed. "I can't really say why, but when I walked into that room, I knew that I had to try to help her in any way I could. I just don't know how. That's what I am hoping you can help me with." He knew his voice sounded almost defeated when he talked about this, because as much as he really did want to help her, he just had no clue how to do it.

"I understand Rayne has that effect on people," she said with a smile of admiration. "But I agree, it isn't going to be easy. Trust me, I've tried. But maybe together we can figure out something to do."

"Well, I promised you a beer, so please, choose anything you want from the menu. It's all my treat," he said, gesturing to the menu.

"Ah, padding the expense report, huh?" she said with a devilish smile. Walt liked this girl; she had some attitude and a great sense of humor.

"Nah," he said, chuckling. "I know the owner; I get a discount."

Sunni made her choices from the menu, but her mind was telling her that this guy was someone she really liked. Not "liked liked," but she did think that maybe his humor and seeming love of life just might help her friend. "So, what would you like to know?" she asked.

"Well, I pretty much know the facts of the case, the clinical ones at least. I have the reports, I understand the accident. I also know that her doctor and her therapist seem to think that she really isn't interested in trying to get better. I just don't understand why. I know she was a great dancer and that is not something she will ever be able to go back to. I am sure that is devastating, but I don't understand why that seems to have made her give up totally," he admitted.

"Did you talk to her dance instructor?" Sunni asked. Walt nodded in the affirmative. "Well then you understand where she was headed before this accident. She really was on a one-way path to being one of the best in the country. Hell, she already was one of the best in the country; the job in New York would have just been a better opportunity to show that to the world." She paused as if trying to figure out how to say the next part. "What the dance instructor and most likely no one who hasn't known her as a friend for years could know to tell you is why dance means so much to her."

Walt nodded slightly, trying to encourage the woman to continue. He wanted, no, he needed to understand this woman. "You see, her dad was her biggest fan when she was little. Not in the 'dance moms' pushing your child out of some sense of projecting his dreams on her way." She had a sad sort of smile on her face. "When Rayne was little, she wanted to be a ballerina so badly. I don't know, she had seen a ballet somewhere, on television or in a movie or something, and literally since she was like four, that was all she wanted to be. Her dad totally doted on her with it. She was his princess, his ballerina princess. He was at every one of her recitals, he always brought her flowers. Red roses, he always brought her red roses. Every time she performed, he praised her for being the best, for being his 'prima ballerina.'" She paused again, as if this story was hard to tell. "Again, not in an unhealthy way. He never pushed her, he never told her she needed to become anything, but he supported her dreams like not many fathers do. If she needed a new costume for a performance or a recital, he made sure she had the best money could buy. If she wanted to go to some dance camp or some intensive workshop, he made sure she got there. If she had a performance out of town because of a competition or whatever, he took off work if he had to and was there. Usually in the front three rows, cheering her on. He was her biggest fan."

Walt noticed tears forming in Sunni's eyes. He knew this story didn't have a happy ending; he knew her parents were both dead. He waited quietly, not wanting to push Sunni to tell her story any faster than she was ready to do.

Finally, she continued. "You know, there was a time that I was so jealous of her for that. I never got into ballet, it just wasn't my thing. I tried, but I just didn't have the skill. I took other lessons, hip hop and modern dance; they are more my style. But I've never really made anything out of my dance lessons other than to have fun. But to see Rayne's father, always there, always supportive, always doting on her so much, I kind of wished I had a dad like that."

After another pause, Sunni continued, and he could tell the story was getting more and more difficult to tell. "Anyway, when Rayne was eighteen, her dad was diagnosed with cancer. It was advanced by the time they found it. He didn't have much longer to live by the time they knew what he had. For as long as he was able, he continued to be at every performance. Finally, he got to the point that he couldn't go to them, but he always wanted to hear all about them when she came home. He would ask her to show him how she had danced, and she would, a performance for one. When he died, she took a break for a while, a few months maybe. But soon she was back dancing and going at it with even more heart than before. I have watched her perform and always, at the end of every dance, she smiles up toward heaven and closes her eyes. I know in those moments, she is hearing her father's praise. You can see it on her face." By this time Sunni had real tears flowing freely down her face.

Walt was silent for a few minutes, then he just had to ask, "What about her mom? Was she as supportive of the dancing?"

"No, not that she wasn't supportive, I don't mean that she wasn't, but no, she never doted on Rayne for her dancing, she never praised her like her father had. She still encouraged Rayne to dance, but it just wasn't the same." She seemed to be in deep thought. "For a while, I thought maybe the connection of dancing and her dad would get to be too much, but it was almost like she took it as a challenge to do even better, to go even further. She wasn't obsessed in a bad way, not like it was an unhealthy thing, but I think maybe on the dance floor was where she felt like she was still connected to her dad in some way."

Walt nodded. He could understand that. It had been what they shared, it had been their 'thing' and now she didn't have that anymore. Sunni wiped her eyes and continued. "When her mom died, she took it the way you would expect anyone to really. She was sad, she grieved for sure, she still had her dad, and she had her friends, and she had her dance family to surround her and she went through the grieving process as well as any of us could."

They both sat silently, taking nibbles of their food and sips of their drinks for several minutes, both processing what Sunni had just shared. Walt thought of the one other thing that had bothered him about Rayne's room at the center. He wanted to know why her room seemed so clinical. Why she hadn't had any personal items. "I noticed that her room is literally as lifeless as her eyes seem," Walt noted. "I passed other rooms, and some people have curtains and bedding and other things that I assume they brought from home. Why hasn't anyone brought anything for Rayne to make her room homier? She is going to be there for a while, isn't she? I would have thought someone would have brought some of her personal belongings to her."

"Oh, believe me…" Sunni said. Her voice seemed like an odd combination of sadness and defensiveness. "We have tried. I offered to bring anything from home, but she turned me down. I often bring books or magazines for her. Offering to leave them for when she gets bored. I shy away from anything having to do with entertainment. I don't want to remind her of what she can't have. But I've taken it all, books of poetry, magazines about anything and everything except entertainment. I've taken crosswords and word search; I've offered to bring her pillow or her sheets. You name it, I've offered. The only things she has asked me to bring are her hairbrush, toothbrush and a few other personal items like that. She won't let me bring anything that might brighten up the room. She won't even keep the magazines I bring. When she was getting get well cards at the beginning, she would ask me to open them and read them. She would acknowledge that someone had sent it, but she wanted me to take them with me when I left. She basically acts like she wants to just sit in that room with nothing but the four walls and a window to stare at." Again, she seemed so sad for her friend.

Finally, after the food was gone, the drinks consumed and the conversation began to drag, Walt realized that he didn't want to keep the woman any later than it already was. She had stayed much longer than he had expected her to, and she had given him a lot to think about. He had one last question for her, though. "I know it's late, and I really appreciate your time and all the information you have shared with me tonight. Her dance coach told me that she feels that dance somehow plays a part in Rayne's recovery. Do you agree with that?"

Sunni pondered that for a while before answering, "Honestly, I can see what she means. I think if Rayne could be involved in dance somehow, it might bring some life back to her, but I can't tell you how to get her to agree to that. I don't think she will willingly be involved with dance in any capacity right now, and most likely not ever again."

"I understand and I thank you so much for what you have shared with me tonight. Please, if you think of anything else that might be helpful, don't hesitate to call." He stood and helped her out of her chair. "I'm sure we will be in touch as the litigation goes forward."

"Thank you, for dinner and for letting me share my thoughts. I sometimes feel like I'm just worthless when it comes to helping Rayne. And, as much as I want to just shake her and tell her that she needs to want to have more of a life than sitting staring out a window, I can't do that because I know it has to come from somewhere inside of her."

Walt walked Sunni out to her car and thanked her again. He was ready to go home; this had been a long day. He was up early, and now it was getting late. But really, it wasn't the number of hours that made him feel weary. He was sure it had a lot more to do with the emotional conversation he had shared with Sunni. He walked back in long enough to grab his briefcase from the office and to let Jason know that he was headed out. As he walked past the bar area, the stupidest idea came to him. When they had decided on the name for their brewery, they had decided they needed a mascot of sorts. Behind the bar were all sorts of things with their name and logo on them. Beer mugs, shot glasses, T-shirts and the goofiest looking stuffed sloth he had ever seen. It was wearing a Five Sloths Brewing T-shirt. "Hey, Jas, hand me one of those sloths, will ya?" he asked his partner.

Jason looked at him like he was a little crazy, but then handed one of the stuffed toys across the counter. As Walt started to walk away, Jason said, "Hey, that will be fourteen ninety-five!" Walt turned to make sure no patrons were watching, and he gave Jason his happy middle finger before turning and walking out the door. Who knows, maybe a stupid looking sloth with an even more stupid T-shirt would help to break the ice with one beautiful ballerina.

Chapter Five

Walt was at the rehab facility early Monday morning. He knew that Rayne had an appointment with her therapist. He hoped that he could bullshit his way into being able to sit in on that session. He planned to tell her that observing might give him more insight to just what her injuries were and would help him better represent her in court if he saw just how she was affected. What he wouldn't tell her was that he wanted to see how she reacted; just how much did she try to be proactive in her own healing process? Did she participate at all? Or did she only do the things that machines or other people basically did for her?

He knocked at her door and waited for her to allow him in. He held that stupid sloth. Who knows, she might laugh at him, although probably not; that would require her to show some emotion. She might throw it at him and tell him to get out and never try anything so stupid again. But he also doubted that; it would require her to show some emotion too. The far more likely scenario was that she would just let it sit there, most likely until Sunni came again and she would ask her friend to dispose of the silly thing.

"Come in," Rayne said quietly from inside her room.

"Good morning, Rayne," Walt said, stepping through the door. He gave her a bright smile, at least wanting her to see that he was happy to see her.

"Oh, hello," she said, she seemed rather surprised to see him, although the surprise that registered briefly on her face was gone in seconds and the hollow look returned.

"Hi," Walt said. Why did he feel nervous? He'd never felt nervous with a client before. "I uh, I was hoping that you wouldn't mind if I came to your therapy session today," he said.

"Why?" she asked, her brow furrowed slightly. Well, confusion was at least an emotion. He had gotten something out of her at least.

"Uh, I just thought that maybe if I sit in a time or two, I might get a better feel for what your injuries are. I would have an idea of what you are going through so that when we get to litigation, I can better argue your case."

"Oh, okay." She shrugged her shoulders. "They usually come to take me down in about fifteen minutes."

Good. That would give him a few minutes to talk to her—that is, if she would talk to him at all. He noticed her looking oddly at what was in his hand.

"Oh, uh—" Why was he saying 'uh' so much? He was a star litigator who had argued in front of some of the toughest judges in the state. He shouldn't be struggling so badly with what to say to this petite woman. But something inside him told him that this was the argument that mattered. These were the words of his own lifetime. Something inside of him needed to fix this woman. No, that wasn't right, he couldn't fix anything for her, but he hoped with everything that he had that he could make her want to fix herself. "I brought you a little something. It's kind of silly really, but I kind of feel like I'm going to be getting all up in your business for the next few weeks because, actually, I am. I am going to be prying into so much of your situation that I thought maybe it was only fair to tell you a little bit about me too. A quid pro quo as we say." He looked at her and she still seemed to be staring at him blankly. Either she had no clue what he was talking about or she just didn't care. He just wasn't sure which it was.

"Yeah, so, uh, anyway. This is Sigma the sloth. Silly name I know. Silly creature actually, but anyway..." he continued. *Wow, way to sound intelligent there, Walt*, he chided himself. "My former frat brothers and I run our own microbrewery here in town and for reasons that make absolutely no sense, Sigma here is a mascot of sorts for the brewery. I'll have to take you there sometime. We serve some really great food." She still seemed to be just staring at him. Maybe she wasn't sure she would ever go anywhere. Whether it was not wanting to go with him or her doubt that she would ever see the outside of this facility, he wasn't sure. *Oh well, in for a penny...as they say*. He rambled on. "He's wearing a T-shirt with the information of our place on it. If you ever can't get ahold of me, someone there will most likely know how to. Anyway, I just thought that maybe he could be here to keep you company." With that, he set the sloth on the small table near the window where she always sat. That was how to do it, just leave it here. Not ask her if she wanted it. If she didn't want it, he had no doubt she could have Sunni or even some nurse dispose of it. He felt awkward as the silence between them seemed to grow and grow.

He had to say something, so he said the first thing that came to his mind. "I would be glad to escort you down to the therapy room, save the orderly or whatever the trip." He added, "That is, if you don't mind. I'm going that way anyway." He tried to make it sound humorous, like there was no pressure and there was no reason for her to say no.

"All right," she agreed. He got behind her wheelchair and started down the hall toward the therapy rooms on the other side of the building.

Trying to make the trip seem less awkward than it had started, he asked her about different aspects of the case. Like how long she thought she would be here—she didn't know, it was up to her doctor and therapist. Did she feel the staff here provided her with adequate care?— her only answer to that was "it's fine." So she wasn't going to give him much to go on here. He had a feeling that getting her to give a statement was going to be like a dentist trying to pull impacted wisdom teeth.

Finally, they arrived at the therapy room and headed toward the young woman he had talked with the other day. She turned when she heard them approaching and surprise registered on her face when she saw who was behind Rayne's chair. He needed to get ahead of this one and quickly. "Hi. I was hoping you wouldn't mind if I sit in on a session here and there. It would really help me to get a feel for what we need to put into the final complaint." He was totally bullshitting and he had a feeling that the therapist knew that somehow.

"Is that okay with you, Rayne?" she asked, looking at her client.

"It's fine with me," Rayne said quietly.

"Well then," the therapist said, looking up at Walt. He looked at her over Rayne's head and mouthed the word "please." Maybe she could see that this wasn't necessarily professionally necessary, but he thought that maybe she could see that he had the best of intentions for being there. "If Rayne is fine with it, then I am fine with it, but I do need you to stand back near the wall, so you aren't in anyone's way." Again, he mouthed a "thank you" before taking his place near the wall.

He watched for the entire forty-five-minute session. It was excruciating to watch. Not that it seemed to be causing her physical pain. It just seemed like she wasn't invested at all. When she was hooked to a machine that did the work for her, she let the machine do it all; she didn't seem to try to add any effort other than just limply letting it take her where it wanted her to go. She seemed to relax when she was attached to anything that added heat or massage. But she didn't seem to enjoy it; again, it was something to be endured. When the therapist asked her to push with her feet or to try a movement completely on her own, she gave it a halfhearted effort if she gave it any effort at all. She just was not participating in her own healing process in any way. It saddened him to see the woman that he had watched in all those videos jumping and spinning in ways that amazed him basically giving up on trying even the most basic of movements. Something had to change, he knew that; he just didn't know how to make it happen. When she was finished with her session, he asked if she would mind if an orderly took her back to her room, since he had a few more questions for the therapist. All in the interest of giving her the best representation as possible, of course. When she was out of the room completely, he turned to the therapist. She seemed to look as lost as he felt.

"Well, now you see for yourself," she said. "She just has no desire to participate at all."

"Are you absolutely certain that it's not that she can't physically?" he asked. If that were the case, then there was some hope that with time could come more healing. But he was pretty sure he knew the answer to that one before he even asked it.

"Yes" the therapist said through clenched teeth. "I am absolutely certain; I have seen her x-rays and other tests. There is no physical reason she isn't standing on her own by now."

"Woah, sorry, I didn't mean to sound like I was challenging your ability," he apologized. "I guess I was just hoping that it was physical at this point. I don't want to know that she has given up. I understand that it seems she has, but that doesn't mean that I want to know it."

That seemed to appease the young woman somewhat. At least she wasn't glaring daggers at him anymore. "Yeah, sorry. I shouldn't get so defensive. I get it. You just want the best for her like all of us do."

"One more question, if I haven't offended you beyond reason" he said. At her nod, he proceeded. "Her dance coach told me that she feels that somehow dance is the answer to Rayne's loss of hope. That somehow dance has to be a part of her healing process." He could see the skeptical look on the woman's face. Of course Rayne couldn't dance; he knew that. Before she could object, he rushed on. "I know that she can't dance, she will never dance the way that she did in the past, I just mean that she feels that somehow dance is the answer. Does that give you any ideas?"

The therapist pondered what he said for a few minutes before answering. "Actually, there might be something to that. I don't know, it's something I have heard of, but never done. Let me investigate it some more. There may be some articles that I can send you that might give you some help in that area."

"Great. Here's my card, email me anything that you think may help." He handed her a card and walked out of the room.

Walt headed back to Rayne's room. He at least wanted to say goodbye, let her know that he was leaving. He wasn't sure if she cared or not, but he wanted to do it anyway. He knocked lightly and waited. Not that he thought she would be doing anything private, but he didn't ever want her to feel like he didn't totally respect her space, even if it didn't really seem like she had made it her space. When he heard her soft "come in," he entered the room. She was sitting looking out the window again, the same place he had found her that first day. The sun was shining in and her auburn hair showed the flecks of red and gold that made it even more beautiful. For a moment, Walt couldn't breathe. She looked almost like an angel sitting there with the halo of light surrounding her. He mentally scolded himself for losing his train of thought and stepped farther into the room. He noticed that stupid sloth sitting on the table beside her. It wasn't in the same position he had put it in. Had she picked it up? Had she maybe felt some sort of emotion about the thing? Even if it was curiosity or disgust, he would take it. The thing wasn't the cutest stuffed animal in the world. If it had gotten any sort of feeling from her, it was at least a step in the right direction. It was something.

Of course, he might be totally off base. Maybe some housekeeper had moved it to dust in here; maybe she hadn't been the one to move it at all. He knew it was very likely the thing would disappear as soon as he was out the door. But at least a part of him had hope that it had gotten some sort of reaction from her.

"I just wanted to stop by and let you know that I'm taking off," he said. "I need to get back to the office. We have some experts coming in this week so that we can get an idea of how to go forward." She nodded her understanding. "I'll be back in the next few days and fill you in on where we are at." He hesitated. He didn't want to say goodbye to her, but he didn't know what reason he had to stay other than the fact that he wanted to. He wanted to talk to her, and not about the case. He wanted to look at her beautiful face and try to find any spark of life in her eyes. But that would probably make him seem like a creeper, so he had to say goodbye—for now. "Take care, and if you need anything don't hesitate to call."

"Of course," she said as he walked away, and he watched her turn her head back out the window. What was it that she saw out there? He had looked and there was nothing out of the ordinary in his viewing. But she saw something out there, even if it was all imagined on her part. That gave him an idea. He smiled as he walked out of the facility. A new plan—now to figure out just how to put it in place.

After Walt left, Rayne picked up the stuffed sloth. It wasn't the most beautiful of stuffed animals. It looked kind of wrinkly and pathetic, but then again, it was a sloth, after all. Still, it was the first gift she had ever gotten from a "boy." No, she didn't think of Walt as a boy. But her dating life had been nonexistent, so this was a first. She knew Walt hadn't given her the stuffed toy as a grand romantic gesture; he had most like just been trying to make her feel more at ease with him, but still... it was her first gift from a boy!! She held the sloth to her chest and stared back out the window. It was too bad that she hadn't met Walt when she had been a whole person. Maybe they could have gone on dates or something. Maybe he would have kissed her goodnight. Maybe there could have been more. But she was pretty sure that there wouldn't ever be "more" for her.

Chapter Six

That afternoon Walt's assistant told him he had a call waiting from Sunni. Ah, good, she had gotten his message and was returning his call. "Sunni, hi, thanks for getting back to me so quickly," he said as soon as the phone was to his ear. He usually took calls on speaker, but for some reason, this whole thing felt more like something he didn't want anyone to overhear.

"No problem," she said. "You sounded like you needed some information from me so I called as soon as I could."

"I do. I need some information. Can you tell me if there was ever anything that Rayne liked, something not having to do with dance?" He knew he wasn't asking this right. She probably thought he was going a little crazy. "Look, I'm not asking this right. I guess, for example, some people love kittens, some love butterflies, or dragonflies. That type of thing. Was there ever anything that Rayne really liked? But it must have nothing to do with dance. I want this to be a happy thing, not a thing that reminds her of her pain more than just surviving already does."

She was quiet for a few moments, apparently either thinking about her answer or thinking about how to get this obvious stalker off her friend's case and finding an attorney who wasn't slightly obsessed with the client. Finally, she apparently decided that he wasn't too much of a creeper and that she could answer. "Rainbows," she said. "You know with the name Rayne, rainbows always seemed to be her thing. When we were younger, she had them on things like her folder in school and all over her room. Why do you ask?"

"Oh, just an idea that I had. I thought maybe I could find something that she would want in her room. I don't know, maybe it's crazy of me to try," he muttered.

"No, it's not crazy," Sunni objected. "It's actually really sweet of you."

"Okay, well, I'm not sure exactly how I am going to go about this, but it's an idea at least," he said. "I'll let you go for now. That was all I needed."

He started to hang up the phone when he heard Sunni start to speak. "Hey, Walt, thanks for caring about my friend. I don't know if she will ever see it, or if she will ever care, but I appreciate the fact that you seem to care about her." He could hear a slight hitch in her voice, like maybe she was getting choked up over this topic. "It means a lot to her, even if she can't tell you that right now." Walt waited until Sunni hung up, just in case she had more to say. He wasn't even sure how to respond, but it did make him feel good that her friend thought he was doing something helpful.

Two days later, Walt sat in the parking lot of the rehab facility. Zak pulled up and got out of his car and into Walt's car. "Okay, so why am I here at the ass crack of dawn?" Zak asked.

"First of all, it's not the ass crack of dawn. It's almost 9 a.m.—you know, the time that you are supposed to be starting your workday. And second, you are here because I need a favor," Walt explained.

He had searched the Internet for the perfect thing to use for the next step of his plan. And he had picked it up the night before. The problem was, he couldn't do the next part himself. He might get caught, but he could go inside and keep Rayne busy while his friend put the plan in motion. "See that window, the one with the white curtain, third one down?" he asked.

"Yeah, I see it. What about it?" Zak asked skeptically. "Look, dude, I'm not going to turn into a peeping Tom here, am I? Not that I mind watching certain things, but I'm not sure a place like this would look too kindly on me looking into a patient's window."

"No, asshole." That was his affectionate term for Zak. "I'm not asking you to be a peeping Tom. I want you to take this wind chime and hang it in the tree that is right outside that window. I need it to be visible from that window. I called the staff, it's totally okay to have wind chimes outside of the patient rooms."

"And you can't put it there, why?" he asked.

"Because I don't want her to know that I put it there. I want her to think that maybe the staff just decided to hang them around the building or something." He ran his hand through his hair, not sure how to explain this to his best friend. "Look, just wait for like fifteen minutes and go put it in that tree. That will give me enough time to make sure she isn't in the room and is out for therapy. It means a lot to me; I can't really explain why."

Zak looked at him for a moment then got all serious like. "Okay," he agreed. "But you do realize that waiting fifteen minutes before I do this is totally going to make me late for work. Right?"

Walt snorted at that comment. "Yeah, like you've been the poster boy for getting to work on time. I don't think you've been on time since you started with the firm."

"Yeah, well, the pressure of being on time is real, man," Zak joked.

Walt started to get out of his car and turned back to say, "Yeah, whatever you say, douchebag. Just do what I asked."

He could hear Zak laughing as he started to walk away. Then Zak said, "Walt, wait up!"

Walt turned back to see what the asshole wanted now. "Just wanted to tell you that I think it's really sweet you are doing all this for your girlfriend," Zak said.

"She's not my girlfriend," Walt began to protest, but Zak just raised an eyebrow then looked at him with the obvious "Really dude, you're going there?" look on his face.

"Okay, yeah, whatever. So I care about this girl," Walt agreed. Zak just gave him a big grin.

When Walt pushed Rayne's chair back into her room after another failed therapy session, he knew he owed his friend, big time. Not only was the wind chime in perfect sight right outside of her window, but he had placed it perfectly for the morning sun. It not only had rainbows on each dangling piece, but hanging below that rainbow was a raindrop-shaped prism. The sun was reflecting rainbows all over the walls of her room. So not only had he given her rainbows to look at outside, along with a soft beautiful sound if her window happened to be open, he had succeeded in filling her room with some color, at least in the morning hours when the sun was on that side of the building. He was feeling satisfied with himself when her head shot up and she started looking at the walls of her room. "What the....." She didn't sound overly pleased as she wheeled herself over to her window.

She was looking up into the tree, probably wondering how the heck that had gotten there when he stepped beside her. "Oh," he said, sounding surprised. "Well, that's a nice touch. I'll bet the facility put them up in various places to add some color. Either that or your next-door neighbor put it there. Maybe that's it." He knew he was grasping at straws here, but there was another window that technically shared that same tree. It could be their wind chime after all...right? And, if he read

Rayne correctly at all, he knew she wouldn't make a fuss over something that was put there for someone else. If it were put there for her, she might object, but if it was there for the person in the neighboring room, she would never be so rude as to ask to have it removed. At least, that was what he was banking on. When he left, he mentally gave himself a high-five. The sloth was still there, and this time, it was sitting on her bed. She was at the very least keeping it nearby, maybe even holding it and gaining some form of comfort from it.

As soon as Walt got back to his office, he scanned his emails for the one from Rayne's therapist. During the therapy session she had alluded to the fact that she had forwarded that "medical information" he had asked for to his email address that morning. Walt had politely thanked her verbally but had made sure that only she could see the true gratitude on his face. He only hoped that the information contained within that email would give him some sort of idea of what else he could do.

He read article after article of how dance in various forms could be used as a therapy of sorts. Especially in cases where there was at least a good range of motion left in the patient. He knew that Rayne would never be a prima ballerina again, but maybe, just maybe she could find a way to let dance be a part of her life again. The problem was, he didn't know how to dance, and he really didn't want it to be anyone else who gave her this. "Paula," he said into the intercom system. When his admin responded, asking what he needed, he answered simply, "Find a dance studio that's close by and teaches ballroom dancing." If she thought that was an odd request, she had the intelligence and presence of mind to not say anything.

Walt had to buy himself some time and, since he was representing the injured party in the lawsuit, he was the one who could petition the judge for a postponement in the case. All he had to do was say that he needed more time for depositions and research and the judge would most likely go along with it. After all, it wasn't like the construction company was going to push for an earlier trial date. The longer they could put this off, the better it was, in their opinion. It wasn't that he needed any time for what he claimed to the judge. With what he already had it was pretty much an open and shut case. Rayne had been walking down the street, going from her apartment to the small grocery store on the nearby corner. A truck from a construction company had stopped at light with a load of 4-inch metal conduit. The tie straps holding the pipes onto the flatbed of the truck hadn't been strapped down completely and some of the piping had started to roll when the truck came to a stop. The first pipe had basically bowled her legs right out from under her and as she fell back, her hips and lower back had landed on another pipe. She had broken a few bones, but those had been clean breaks and were healing well. It was the muscle and nerve damage that had really caused the problem. That was what would take her actively participating in her therapy to get better. Somehow, he needed to get her to want to get better.

He began dance lessons, and at first, it seemed kind of awkward. Going alone as a single man probably seemed odd to the other students. One night when the class was ending, the female instructor asked him if she could have a moment. He wondered if she was going to tell him that he wasn't good enough to be in her class. On the contrary, she asked him why exactly he was taking the class. Was he preparing for a wedding or possibly some other event> He hesitated and then began to tell her the truth of his motivation. She listened to his story and when he was done, she was smiling. "That's very admirable of you," she said. "However, I would argue that she isn't simply a client to you." Exactly what she was, or even what he wanted her to be wasn't fully clear to him, but yes, she was more than simply a client. "I can't argue with that," he admitted.

"I have a suggestion for you, if I may," she said. "I think these lessons aren't really the best for what you are seeking. I would suggest that we begin working privately, I have some suggestions that I think might help you to help your client." Walt agreed to the change; he would try anything if it would help Rayne.

It was the best suggestion anyone could have made. What he hadn't realized was that the instructor was familiar with the ideas of dance being used as therapy. She helped him find an apparatus that he could use to strap Rayne's feet to his so that until she had the strength to move her legs into the positions needed, he could do the movements for her. Or she could start on her own steam and add the straps if she was getting to fatigued to continue. He learned several types of ballroom dancing. Two weeks after that first lesson, he by no means considered himself a dancer, but he hoped that maybe he knew enough to help Rayne find her way back to being among the living.

He called Sunni and asked her if she would come to the brewery again. He needed to get her input on how to put his plan into motion. She agreed to meet him later that evening.

When she walked in, he gave her a smile and waved her over to the same table they had sat at before. He was anxious to tell her his plan. He began telling her about the research that he had gotten from the therapist and the fact that he had taken dance lessons just to try to help Rayne. He just wasn't sure how to get her to cooperate. He knew he had rambled through his whole speech, probably not making any sense at all. But he hoped she would see that he was really, really interested in trying help. When he got done, he took a breath and waited to see what her reaction would be.

She appeared to be speechless. Was it really that horrible of an idea? Finally, she took pity on him and spoke. "Oh my, God." Okay, here it went, she was going to tell him what an idiot he was. "Oh, my God," she repeated shaking her head. "I can't believe you would do that. I've never heard someone go so far to help someone they barely even know. How, why would you...." She was still shaking her head, amazed, then suddenly her eyes went wide, and she said, "Oh my God, you love her!"

He wasn't sure he would go that far; it wasn't love. He tried to backpedal. "Well, I wouldn't say love. I'm not sure that I've ever been in love, but I do care. I do want her to get better. I want to see life in her eyes."

"Well, you may not consider it love, but whatever you call it, you have done so much for my friend that I don't even know how to thank you." She looked like she was going to cry. "I saw the sloth that you gave her. She tried to pass it off as something silly that you had left there, and she hadn't wanted to be rude and throw it away. But every time I go there, it's in a different spot. One time when I walked in, she quickly set it on the table like she hadn't been holding it just before I got there. You put up the wind chime too, didn't you?"

"I—well, no, I didn't actually put that up..." he wasn't sure how to handle all this emotion.

"You may not have physically put it there, but you did it, it was you, I knew it had to be when I walked into her room that day and saw rainbows all over the wall."

"Yes, I had hoped it would give her some sort of joy."

"I don't know that she will ever admit it, or say anything, but even if she isn't acknowledging it openly, that wind chime has to be something she enjoys," Sunni encouraged.

"I have something else I am hoping to do, and I was wondering if you would be willing to be my partner in crime. I would really like to get Rayne to come out here with me for dinner. I am hoping that she will be wined and dined to the point that I can convince her to maybe dance with me, just a little." He sounded almost shy because he really didn't know if this plan would work. "I thought maybe I could invite the both of you, I could even have one of my partners be your date for the evening. I doubt I could convince her to come on her own, but maybe if you brought her..." He hesitated. "I don't know, maybe it's a really stupid idea. She may not go for it at all."

"It can't hurt to try. I will work it from my end, and you work it from yours. Maybe between the two of us we can convince her to at least get out for one evening. Convincing her to dance is all on you, though. I am not sure that will be possible," Sunni replied.

Chapter Seven

On Friday, Walt stopped by Rayne's room. He had thought about bringing flowers or something, but that seemed like maybe a little over the top. So he just took some file folders so he could use work as an excuse to see her again. He did need to discuss some things with her. They could have waited till Monday, but he wanted to see her today to hopefully set his plan in motion. Sunni would be here on Saturday as usual and they had already agreed that she would encourage the night out from her end of things. Oddly enough, Sunni had agreed to the plan with the stipulation that her "date" be "the hot bartender" from the first night she had been there. And of course, Jason had not objected at all to the double date when he realized his escort was the hot blond girl.

"Hi," Walt said after she had told him to come in. "I had some things I wanted to go over with you, if you have time."

"I have nothing but time it seems," she sulked. The sloth was on the floor by her bed, like maybe she had tried to toss it when someone had knocked, and it hadn't landed right. It didn't look like it had been cast aside; it looked more like her aim had been off.

"Speaking of which," he began—*Great segue there, Walt*—"I was hoping maybe you would want to come to dinner with me on Monday night. I would really like to show you my brewery. You know that Sunni and I have met, and it seems she thinks one of my partners is 'hot.'" He actually did the air quotes. "Anyway, Mondays the pub is closed to the general public, so you wouldn't have to deal with crowds or loud rowdy patrons. It could just be the four of us. It might give you some insight into who I am when I'm not in lawyer mode." He was rambling, he knew he was, but he just couldn't stop. This was too important to him for her to not say yes. However, she looked totally bewildered by his insane rambling. Finally, he decided to work it from plan B. "Well, you don't have to answer right now. Why don't you talk it over with Sunni and see if that is something the two of you would enjoy? You can let her or me know if you decide you want to have dinner."

Rayne was totally thrown off. What was happening? Was he asking her on a date, or was he just wanting to have time outside of the facility to discuss her case? She had to admit it wasn't the warmest of places. He was probably just getting tired of meeting her in a sterile hospital type environment. "Okay, I... I'll talk to Sunni and we can let you know," she finally stammered.

Walt went on with discussing some of the aspects of her case, but she really wasn't sure all of it registered in her brain. She was still trying not to be obvious and pinch herself in front of him. Hopefully he wasn't asking her any questions that were going to make or break her case because if he was, she probably blew the whole thing.

Chapter Eight

The next day, Rayne was sitting in her chair by the window, enjoying the rainbow prisms all over her wall when her friend arrived. She was dying to get her friend's take on what Walt had asked her yesterday. She felt almost like a schoolgirl with a crush and did not want to be reading this wrong. She needed Sunni to be the logical one and tell her that it most likely was just a change in scenery that Walt was hoping for.

"Hey, girlfriend," Sunni said brightly when she walked in. She, too seemed to be looking around the room at all the rainbows. "Wow, I don't get here this early most of the time. This time of day that thing really lightens up this room! It's gorgeous in here."

"Yeah, it really is," Rayne agreed. "Look, Sunni, I have to ask you something, and I need you to be brutally honest with me, okay?" Her friend looked a little nervous at what she was asking, but she nodded her assent. "Okay, so Walt asked me to go to his pub for dinner Monday night. He said you had agreed to bring me with you, something about your liking the hot bartender or something. So, I must know, do you think he is wanting to discuss my case in a less clinically boring facility, or do you think it's something else?"

Sunni shook her head, "Girl, listen to yourself, look at yourself, think for all of two seconds. This man has come here at least two or three times a week. Has he always been completely about business?"

"Well, yeah, mostly.... I mean.... I don't know," she said softly.

"Uggghh!! ,Rayne look at me! I know that sloth came from him. I know he comes here and claims to be 'observing your therapy' or whatever. I shouldn't say this, but here goes. He is not asking you to dinner so he can question you about your case. He asked you to dinner because he is interested. And not in how much he can get for the case." Sunni's frustration was very evident on her face. "This man likes you. Look, I know you were so busy with life that you haven't dated and haven't ever had a guy want to buy you things. But trust me, this is him wanting to get to know you better as a person, as a woman, not simply as a client."

"Really?" Rayne almost wanted to cry. This was a first. "But why? I mean, I'm nothing, I can barely walk, I'm a nobody."

Sunni grabbed the handles of Rayne's wheelchair and spun her around so she was facing the mirror over the dresser. "Because you are beautiful, damn it!! You are a gorgeous woman. He's not blind. Just because you are in a chair right now doesn't mean that you always must be. Fight for this, please, for me, for yourself. Fight to get better and fight for a chance to see what can really happen if you open yourself up to this man."

"Okay, I'll try." She was scared to death to try, but, maybe, just maybe there was life after death after all. "But I have no idea what to wear," she lamented.

"Oh, now, you are talking!! That's the Rayne I know and love. We got some planning to do, girlie." Sunni spun her back around and sat in the chair across from her. "So, let's see, it's a pub, so jeans are totally appropriate. However, it's a hot guy so, ya know, tight jeans." She smiled and raised her eyebrows. "We will get you looking like you are so ready for a night on the town."

"But, I'm not, not really. I can't wear heels or anything. Sunni, I can barely walk."

"Heels not required, flats are fine. It's the tight jeans and maybe a little cleavage that will have him hooked. And as far as walking, I don't think that will be an issue either. You can take a few steps into the car from your chair, and we will work out the rest when we get there." Sunni sure seemed to have this all planned out, Rayne thought.

By Monday morning Rayne was both excited and nervous. When she got to therapy, she pushed herself. She finally thought that there might just be a reason to be able to walk again. Maybe, just maybe a boy liked her, she thought with a smile. After therapy was over, she went back to her room to shower and begin to get ready for her date. She still couldn't believe that she was going on a date and with a hot guy, too. She felt like this had to be a dream, but every time she pinched herself, it hurt, so no, not a dream, then. She didn't want to push herself too much before the date, so for the most part, she still did everything from her wheelchair, only standing when necessary for dressing or to reach something. She could take some steps, but after pushing herself at therapy, she wanted to save what strength she could for hopefully not making a total fool of herself tonight. She didn't want to be the pathetic girl when she was out with the hottest guy in town. At least he was in her opinion.

When Sunni arrived, she pulled up under the awning that covered the front entrance. She went in to find Rayne waiting right by the door in her chair. She was obviously anxious for this night. When she started to wheel Rayne out to the car, the nurse asked, "Are you going out tonight, Rayne?" She looked at Sunni a little bewildered. No one had ever seen Rayne want to do much more than leave her room.

"Yes, I am. I have a date," Rayne said with a smile.

"It wouldn't be with that handsome attorney that you have had hanging around here, now would it?" the nurse teased.

"Well, um, yes, it is," Rayne said shyly.

"Oh, well, in that case, have fun, and remember, the door's open 24/7. There's no reason to rush on our account. We'll be here." As Rayne turned away, Sunni could see the big smile on the nurse's face, and she gave Sunni a big thumbs-up.

Rayne had not had a problem getting into Sunni's car. She had pulled right up to the door. The problem had come in the fact that Rayne's chair wouldn't fit in Sunni's tiny car. Rayne was nervous about how that would work out when they got to the pub.

"I'll just text Walt and let him know we are on our way. I know the pub isn't open tonight, so I should probably give him a heads-up that it will be us," Sunni said.

Walt felt his phone vibrate with a text and pulled it out of his pocket. He had been pacing for the last half hour. Jason was totally giving him shit about being nervous, but he didn't care. Tonight was important to him. The text was from Sunni; his girl was on her way to him. At least he hoped she would be his girl.

On our way, chair wouldn't fit in my car though

No problem

"Hey, Jase, the girls are on their way, but they couldn't bring Rayne's wheelchair, so I'm going to watch for them so I can help her get in okay," he said on his way to the front door. The pub wasn't open, but he had gotten the cook to come in to make whatever they wanted to have for dinner. He stepped out into the main foyer and watched for the headlights of Sunni's car. *Here goes,*' he thought to himself when he saw them turn into the parking lot. *This will either gain me brownie points or show her that I'm a total creeper.* Hoping for the best, he walked out to meet the girls just as Sunni turned off the engine.

Sunni stepped out and looked at Walt over the car with a bit of a concerned look on her face. He could tell she wasn't sure how the 'no chair' thing was going to go over. In Walt's mind, it wasn't an issue. He simply got to hold his girl sooner rather than later. Or not rather than; he sincerely hoped he would be holding her both now and later.

He opened Rayne's door and smiled at her brightly. "I hear we had an issue with space and the proportions of this car. I am here to be of service, my lady," he said with an exaggerated bow.

"Oh, um, well, I can probably walk, if someone can help me," Rayne said nervously.

"I'm sure you can, sweetie, but I'd really rather you not push yourself too much. We have a whole night ahead of us. Besides," he said as he bent and put one arm under her knees and the other against her back, "this gives me an opportunity to hold you."

She started to protest as he picked her up and headed for the door, but Sunni was standing there holding the door open with a big smile and she gave Rayne a small shake of her head that told Rayne it really shouldn't be a big deal. He was only helping her because she didn't have her chair. That was all. There was no reason to read anything more into it than that.

Rayne was thoroughly enjoying herself. The food was so good. It had been a long time since she had had much besides the food at the rehab facility. Sure, Sunni sometimes brought a pizza or some fast food, but this food, this was food that she had rarely ever allowed herself to engage in. The calories and grease in these burgers were probably enough to clog her arteries right on the spot. But, for one night, she didn't care. She was enjoying herself. The conversation was light, pretty much what you would expect from four people who were just getting to know each other. Just basic talking and laughing. Especially when Jason and Walt got to ragging on each other over silly things. Rayne could tell that they had been friends for a long time. As the meal began to wind down, Rayne asked how the brewery had gotten its name.

"Ugh, that is a story that I don't need to hear twice," Sunni said with mischief in her eyes. "How about you give me a tour of this place, Jason?" She smiled sweetly at him.

"I would love to do that," Jason said, practically jumping out of his chair. The two excused themselves and headed toward the back of the bar.

Walt told her the whole story: the frat brothers, the overachievers, that thought the name would be sort of ironic. She was amazed at the accomplishments of this man. He couldn't be more than in his late 20s, yet here he was, a successful attorney, part owner in a business. What was she? She was nothing. She was a 'former dancer' who really had nothing to show for her life. She was mulling over the ideas of just what she could possibly do with her life when she heard Walt saying her name. It was obvious it wasn't the first time he had said it either. She had been lost in thought there for a bit.

When she looked up at him, he had a soft smile on his face. "Will you try something for me?" Walt asked softly.

"What would that be?" she asked. What could she possibly do for him? Yes, she had enjoyed their meal together. She enjoyed his company immensely. They hadn't talked about her case; they had just enjoyed the evening and the meal.

"Dance with me," he said.

"I can't. I can't possibly dance," she sputtered indignantly. Who did this man think he was? How could he be so insulting as to ask her to dance with him? Could he not understand that her legs just didn't work that way anymore? Hell, he had been the one that had to carry her in the door, for goodness sakes. She would humiliate herself if she even tried to get up on the dance floor. She was barely able to hold herself up when walking a few steps. Dancing was out of the question.

"Just give it a try, for me?" The look in his eyes really made something stir in her, but honestly, no, she could not possibly dance.

"I can barely hold myself up when walking. I couldn't possibly dance," she said adamantly. "You carried me in the door."

"Then let me hold you up. Let me be your support. You can place your feet on mine or hold me as tightly as you need to." His eyes were pleading with her just as much as his words were.

He looked almost desperate for her to say yes. She thought about it for a minute. She knew that she couldn't dance. This would be more like just letting him hold her closely. That didn't sound bad at all. And it wasn't like the place was crowded and people would be watching. No, the place was basically deserted except for their friends. Maybe she could let herself go and enjoy this. She had always loved music, had always loved swaying to the rhythm. It wasn't like doing so in a hot guy's arms would be a real hardship.

"Why, why does it mean so much to you for me to do this?" She really needed to know why this was so important to him. If it was pity or if it even seemed like pity, she would say no and ask Sunni to take her home immediately.

"I guess because I really want to hold you. I know that you don't believe that you can dance anymore, but I disagree. I think that with the right partner, you could enjoy dancing again. At least try, for me. And if it doesn't work, then I at least got to hold you in my arms for the length of a song or two."

Nope, there was no pity at all behind those eyes. There was hope, there was heat, and maybe even a little bit of arousal in those eyes. What did she have to lose? It would either work, or it wouldn't.

"Okay," she said quietly.

He rose from the table and helped her with her chair. As he had when they came in, he put his arm around her knee and her back and carried her across the room to the small area set up as a dance floor. He nodded to his buddy behind the bar and suddenly soft music surrounded her. It was a musical number, no words. It sounded familiar, but she wasn't sure that she recognized it.

He took her in his arms, the way anyone would do when preparing to do some sort of ballroom dance. "Put your arms around my neck, let me support you. I don't want you to overtax yourself, so lean on me as much as you need to. Put your feet on mine if that is easier."

She did place her feet on his so that he was supporting her weight completely. She wrapped her arms tightly around his neck at first, not at all certain that her legs would hold her for very long. Besides, being this close to Walt would leave any woman weak in the knees.

He placed a hand on each side of her waist, but she could tell that he had complete control of the situation. There was no way he was going to let her fall. So she relaxed her hold slightly. She didn't need to hold on so tightly; he had her. That was an odd feeling, knowing that someone else was there to support her. It wasn't completely about the physical support either. From the conversations of the evening and the way he had treated her, she felt like he supported her personally and emotionally too. Other than her best friend, she hadn't felt like someone had cared this much since her parents had died. She was beginning to fall for this man...hard.

She had never been held by a man, other than brief contact with dance numbers, never been kissed by a man, and had never had sex with a man. So being held so closely to his body was all very new to her. But she had to admit that she really liked it. They began to sway slowly to the music. Not really dancing, but they were both feeling the music and feeling a connection with the other. The more comfortable she got with the way he was holding her, the more she tried to dance. She felt like it really meant something to him for her to be willing to give him this, so she had to at least try. Even if she wasn't any good at it.

But she found that he was making it easy. Her legs, although still very weak and not at all used to this type of movement anymore, started to move along with his a little. She wasn't simply keeping her feet planted on his and going along for the ride. In fact, after a few more moments of gaining confidence, she took her feet off of his and started to move along with him. She still held on tightly and she still relied strongly on his hands supporting her, but she was actually making movements of her own.

She didn't know what felt better, letting the music invade her senses and moving to the rhythm or the way her body was pressed up against his. Either way, this was definitely the best night she had had in a very, very long time. When the song was finished, he just continued to hold her and sway until another song queued up on the system. They changed pace slightly but kept moving in sync with each other and the soothing sound of the music. She placed her head on his shoulder and she could smell his cologne—or maybe it was just him. Regardless of which it was, it was decidedly masculine and very enjoyable to her senses. She closed her eyes and allowed herself to be swept away by the music, his scent and his strong arms around her waist. She had never really been a "ballroom" dance person, but suddenly, it was becoming her favorite type of dance in the world.

As the second song began to wrap up, Walt couldn't help himself anymore. Being this close to her, feeling her body pressed into his, it was just too much. He leaned down and kissed the exposed skin on her neck. With her head on his shoulder, he had perfect access to the back of her neck. She had put her hair up into some sort of a bun, so his access was unhindered. He kissed gently and instantly wanted to taste more of her skin. He kissed slowly, kind of pushing her head in the direction it needed to go for him to have access to the side of her neck and then eventually to her face.

When she started to pull away a bit to look up at him, he leaned down to kiss her softly parted lips. She was so amazingly soft, her skin almost like silk. He loved touching her, he loved kissing her, and he knew he would love to do so much more to her too. His first kiss was gentle, testing to see if she would respond to him or if she would pull away. He didn't put his hand behind her head and draw her closer as he really wanted to do. He wouldn't force this on her. If she wanted to pull back, he would give her every opportunity. But it was she who deepened the kiss. She pressed her mouth more tightly to his. She stretched up more so that they could maintain the contact of their mouths. Walt couldn't take it anymore; he moved his hand from her waist to the back of her head and went for the thing he was craving at this moment. He pushed his tongue against her mouth, hoping that she would open and give him access. And, beautifully, she did. She almost sighed when he opened her mouth to slide his tongue inside. She seemed a little unsure, maybe a little hesitant at first, so he kept the kiss slow and easy. He explored her mouth, but he didn't press harder; he didn't take more than she was willing to offer. When she pulled away a little, he let her. She looked up into his eyes and he wasn't quite sure what he was seeing in hers.

He started to apologize. "Hey, look, sorry about that, I got carried away. It was just that holding you close was so nice and I, uh, yeah, um, sorry." He stammered out the last bit and although he never let her go, or took away his physical support, he decidedly pulled away from her mouth.

"Wait, what? No." What had she done wrong? Why had he stopped kissing her? She had to fix this. "Don't stop, Walt. I don't know what I was doing wrong. I've never been kissed before. Please, I can learn. If you teach me, I will do it better. Just, I really don't want you to stop."

Walt looked at her with amazement in his eyes. "Are you serious? You have never been kissed before?" He couldn't believe no guy had ever tried with her before. Sure, she had always been involved in dancing, but were the guys she met in dance class or at school blind?

She bowed her head like it was something to be ashamed of and shook her head. "No, never," she said quietly.

Walt could tell that she thought that was somehow a bad thing. "Oh, no, sweetheart." He tilted her chin up until her eyes met his. "Don't be ashamed of that. I'm not disappointed. If anything, I am honored that you would let me be your first. You are a beautiful woman, Rayne. I honestly don't know why no man has ever kissed you before, but believe me, you have done nothing wrong. All you have done is make me treasure you more. Please don't hide the real you from me."

He leaned down and started kissing her gently again. If she hadn't been kissed, there was a whole hell of a lot more she hadn't done, and while he definitely hoped he got to be the one to show her all of those things, he was definitely going to have to keep a tight rein on himself so he didn't go too far too fast. She relaxed into his arms again and allowed him to kiss her gently and deeply. He was pretty sure at this point that he was never going to get enough of this woman.

When they finished their dance/makeout session, they turned to go back to the table. It had been cleared and most of the lights had been dimmed. Sunni and Jason were sitting at the bar, having their own rather intimate moment. Rayne looked at Walt and asked if he would mind taking her home. She didn't want to interrupt Sunni and spoil her evening.

"It would be my pleasure," Walt agreed. He looked over to Jason and did some weird sort of head nodding and eye motioning and Jason lifted his chin in acknowledgment of whatever that had all been about and then Walt lifted her again and carried her to the door.

"I can walk some, you know," she said. She tried to sound indignant, but she totally didn't pull it off.

"Oh, I know, I just like holding you." Walt grinned at her as he deposited her into his car. It was a sporty thing, probably worth more than the home her parents had owned when she was growing up. She wished she still had that home in some ways. Although it had been too big for her at the time that she sold it, she now sort of regretted the fact that she lived in a three-story walkup. Even when she could begin to walk more, that apartment was going to be an issue. Oh, well, she would have to worry about that when the time came.

When they got to the rehab facility, her chair was not in the entryway. It had probably been moved to accommodate others, but that left her with the problem of trying to track it down. Walt noticed her looking around and asked, "Something wrong, sweetie?"

She really liked the way he kept using terms like that. "Ah, no, not really, I just don't see any chairs in the entryway. There are usually some there for general use. Mine probably got put back in my room."

"Oh, well, I'd be glad to carry you in, or help you in any way that I can," Walt offered.

As great as it sounded to be carried in his arms again, she really shouldn't impose, and she wasn't sure she wanted both patients and staff seeing her be carried across the threshold of the establishment by a gorgeous hunk of man. "Actually, if you could just walk with me, and support me a little as far as the front desk, I am sure someone there can help me find my chair or get to my room."

"Sure, no problem. Wait there, I'll come around and help you get out," Walt said as he opened his door. He came around and opened her car door like a gentleman would, but then, he reached in and put her arm on his shoulder and his arm around her waist and helped to lift her out of the car. It was like they were dancing again back at the pub. He supported her so much that there was no way she could possibly fall. She felt so secure with this man. She could really get used to this feeling. No, she cautioned herself, that was not the way she should be seeing things. He was nice, he was helping her, he was maybe interested in dating her, but that didn't mean that she should rely on him more than for just the physical support he offered as they walked into the facility together.

When they got inside, there was no nurse at the front desk. This time of night, that wasn't necessarily an oddity. The night shift was shorter staffed, and the front desk wasn't top priority after normal business hours. "Well, that's not what I expected, "she said. "Usually there is a nurse here."

"I can wait here with you, or we can make our way to your room together. I promise I won't let you fall," Walt encouraged.

Somehow it sounded like he was saying he wouldn't let her fall in far more ways than just with helping her walk down a simple hall. "Okay, sure. I don't need to bother the nurse if you are willing to help me," she said.

As they made their way down the hall, Rayne realized that this was much more of an undertaking than she had planned on. With the time she had already spent on her feet dancing, her legs were just done with wanting to cooperate anymore. She stumbled slightly and Walt was right there. He tightened his arm around her and asked her if she was all right. She hated to admit it, but she said, "No, actually, this is getting to be a little too much. I should have gotten my chair."

"It's no problem, sweetheart. Will you let me carry you the rest of the way?" Walt ducked to look into her eyes. Again, there was no pity there, just support and maybe some other feelings too. Dare she hope he was starting to fall for her as much as she was falling for him? She couldn't say anything. There was suddenly a huge lump of emotion in her throat, so she just nodded her assent and Walt bent to pick her up. When he got her to her room, her chair was sitting just inside her door. He gently deposited her into it and got down on one knee, so he was looking directly into her eyes. "Good night, sweetie. I'd like to see you again soon. If that's okay with you?" he asked.

Again, words failed her, but she nodded her assent and Walt leaned in and gave her a gentle kiss on her lips before he turned and walked out the door.

Chapter Nine

Rayne woke in the morning more determined than ever to get better. The night before had shown her that there really was a life out there to be lived. She hoped that maybe that life would include Walt, but, even if it didn't, she realized that there was something more than just sitting within these four walls allowing her muscles to waste away. She was up and ready to go when they came to wheel her down to therapy. When she got there, her therapists were still finishing up with another patient, so Rayne wheeled her way over to the area that was always the first stop: the massage table where heat was applied to get her muscles softened for the day's workout. She got out of her chair and made the few steps to the table and sat herself in place, so she was ready when the therapist was. When they got to the actual exercises, Rayne pushed herself more than she ever had before. Her therapist commented on her increased range of motion. Rayne smiled shyly and said softly, "Well, yesterday, I walked, just a little, and I danced."

The therapist's eyes got big and she asked, "You danced?"

"Yes, well, sort of. It was slow dancing, and he pretty much held me up, so I wasn't really doing much, but yes, I danced." She smiled at the memory.

"Well, good for you!" The therapist was beaming with something, pride maybe, or at least happiness that Rayne was seeming to make progress. "This wouldn't have anything to do with that really good-looking attorney that has been hanging around, would it?" Her voice was easing, but not in a mean way.

"Um, well, yeah, it kind of does." Rayne smiled. "He took me to the pub he co-owns and asked me to dance a little. My friend Sunni drove me there and we sort of had a double date." Uh, yeah, it was kind of awesome being able to say that.... date.... a word she had never used in that context before.

"That's so great. I'm happy to see you getting out and enjoying things. It was obviously good for you; you made more progress today than you ever have before," the therapist encouraged warmly. "It won't be long, and you'll be ready to move to outpatient," Keeley said. Was that a sort of sad face she saw? There was no way that Rayne didn't want to leave here, was there? But when she had mentioned her moving to outpatient there had been a definite look. That was something she would have to check in to. If Rayne was going to take an active part in her sessions from now on, the possibility of moving her to outpatient in the next couple of weeks could be a real option. But something was up. Maybe her attorney would know, or her friend who visited her often. Keeley would have to do some checking. Patients always succeeded far more when they were in their own environment than they did when in the facility, although obviously, sometimes the facility was necessary.

After the session was over, Keeley went to her desk and found Walt's business card. When she was put through to him, she didn't wait for him to say much beyond hello before she told him excitedly, "I don't know what you did, but please keep it up!"

"What do you mean?" Walt asked, puzzled. "This is Keeley, Rayne's therapist, right?" He sounded a little thrown off by her enthusiasm.

"Oh, right, yes, sorry. It's just that I was so excited to tell you that Rayne participated in her session today, I mean like really participated. She has never done this. I asked her what was different. All she said was that she went on a date with you and that she danced. Did you really get her to dance?" she asked.

"Uh, yeah, sort of, it was mostly just swaying back and forth on the dance floor. I supported her weight so that she didn't have to be afraid of falling. So I guess it was dancing of a sort."

"Well, whatever it was, it helped, trust me." She hesitated to say the next part. "But there was another issue, and I'm not really sure what to make of it. I commented that if she made progress like she did today, it wouldn't be long till she could move to outpatient. I'm not sure why, but she didn't really seem overly happy about that. I don't know, maybe I read her wrong."

"Why do you think she wouldn't be happy about leaving?" Walt asked. He did know that sometimes a patient felt safer in a facility. Maybe it was just that she thought that having to take care of everything herself was a bit overwhelming.

"I don't know, and she didn't say anything, it was just sort of a panicked look on her face, I guess," Keeley said.

"Well, I'll talk to Sunni and see if she has any ideas. But thank you for letting me know that therapy went better for her today." Walt hung up the phone, something felt good inside to know that maybe he had played some part in Rayne finally wanting to work at getting stronger. He allowed the good feeling for a moment before picking up his cell phone and calling Sunni. When she answered, he shared the good news about the therapy appointment.

"Well, I can't say I'm really surprised." Sunni responded. "I think you have given her a lot of reason to get better."

"I'm happy that I can. But, listen, Keeley said that when she mentioned that Rayne might be on her way to moving to outpatient therapy, Rayne didn't seem all that happy with the idea. Do you know of a reason that Rayne wouldn't be happy to go home?" Walt asked.

"Oh, shit!" Sunni exclaimed. "I never thought about that. Yeah, I think I know exactly why Rayne wouldn't be happy with it. She lives next door to me, in a third-floor walkup. Damn, why didn't I think about the fact that this would be an issue for her? She won't be able to do three flights of stairs when she gets released. I know she doesn't want to stay in the facility. At least, I don't believe she does anymore. Before I may have thought that because she seemed to have given up. But, no, now I am sure she wants to move out. She just knows that she can't go home. And I live next door, so I am no help," Sunni lamented.

"Ah, I see. Well, that makes sense then. I was hoping that she hadn't become too afraid to be out in the world again. It's just the 'where' she has to be in the world that is an issue." Walt felt like he was taking a step backward for every two he took forward. Yes, Rayne was making progress and that was a great thing, but it seemed like there were still a lot of hurdles to overcome. "Let me think on it for a while," he finally said. "If you think of any solutions, please let me know."

"I will." Sunni sounded almost as defeated as Walt felt.

Walt leaned back in his chair. He had an idea that might work, but, after just one date, he wasn't sure Rayne would be willing to listen. However, even she would have to admit that she didn't have a lot of options. He was going to give it a shot. If she said no, he was going to be out a little money. That wasn't really an issue, but if she said yes, it was going to be worth every single penny. He had some phone calls to make. The one thing he did know, though, was that anything he did had to seem like it wasn't done just for Rayne. She wouldn't agree if she thought he was doing anything specifically for her. It had to seem like it had been there all along.

Chapter Ten

Over the next two weeks, Walt spent several evenings with Rayne, not as her attorney, but hopefully building a friendship and a bond of sorts that would allow him to continue helping her. He generally brought a dinner for them to share, and the evenings always included a few kisses here and there. Rayne seemed comfortable with him. They often touched while talking. Not sexual touches; Walt wasn't going there anytime soon. But small things like putting her hand on his when they talked or placing a hand on her shoulder when he wanted to put her at ease. Rayne smiled more and more all the time.

Finally, all his plans were finished, and he called Sunni and asked her if she would be willing to stop by his house sometime over the weekend. He had an idea to run by her.

"Uh, yeah, okay." Sunni was puzzled about Walt wanting her to stop by his house, but if it was an idea to help Rayne out, then she was all in.

"Just roll with me on this, please. I really need your input," Walt assured her.

"Okay, I'll be there around noon on Saturday if that works for you." Walt confirmed that it was fine, and he gave her his address.

When Sunni pulled up to the gorgeous house on the east side of Grand Rapids, she couldn't help but be envious. She had been pretty sure Walt had money, but she had no idea he had THAT kind of money. As soon as she rang the doorbell, Walt was there opening the door. "Hi! Come on in!" he greeted. As they walked through the foyer, he continued, "Look, I'll get right to the point. I'm sure you are curious why I asked you to come over and to be honest, I'm not sure if what I am thinking is a good idea or not. But I have to try and now I want to know what you think."

Sunni was obviously very puzzled, but she said, "Sure. What is it?"

Walt led her into the kitchen of his spacious home. "So here's my thought. As you can see this house is big and spacious. Too much for a single guy really, but it was a great investment at the time. Anyway, this is the kitchen it has a pretty open floor plan. I have a housekeeper/cook that does all my shopping and she always stocks the freezer and refrigerator with meals that can be warmed in the oven or things that can be heated in the microwave."

Sunni looked around and noted that the kitchen had an 'eat in' area as well as stools at the counter that faced the kitchen. It was a large kitchen. She had never been much of a cook, but if she was, she would love a kitchen like that. She was also sure that the house had a formal dining area, but most likely Walt didn't really use that much. "Uh, yeah, it's a beautiful kitchen, but why are you trying to sell me on the beauty of your home? Are you trying to sell? Because I guarantee, I can't afford this."

"No, just stay with me here," he said. He opened a door that was off the area where the kitchen and living room kind of met. "This is a guest bedroom. It has its own separate end suite bathroom and again, lots of space to move around." Sunni looked the room over and at first, she was still really puzzled why Walt was showing her all this. It wasn't until she noticed the décor that things started falling into place. While the room really could be considered unisex, it wasn't overly feminine or anything. There was a subtle rainbow pattern to the comforter and matching curtains. There was a scenic picture on the wall of a waterfall that had an actual rainbow, but it wasn't the focus of the photo; it was simply a nature scene to most people's eyes. She turned absolutely stunned and looked at Walt. Tears started to form in her eyes. She absolutely could not believe this man. "You did all of this for Rayne, didn't you?"

"Well, the blankets and things, yes. The open floor plan of the house just happens to be a benefit that I think could help her." Walt ran his hands through his hair, like he was kind of shy about what he had done. "I also had an intercom system installed. This box here on the nightstand and the one by the door can contact most other areas of the house, including the kitchen and my bedroom upstairs. I thought it would be helpful if Rayne ever needed any help. I know you said that she really can't go home right now, but my question is, do you think she would come here?"

Sunni took a deep breath and pondered Walt's question. Would Rayne be willing to give up her apartment and independence or not? Would she see the benefit in staying here at least until she was stronger and more certain on her feet, maybe? If the subject was approached properly. And that was what she told Walt. So they put their heads together and tried to plan.

****

Sunni hadn't been to see Rayne yet that day, so she figured she would start to lay the groundwork when she got there that afternoon. It had to sound completely like an awesome idea that Sunni had worked out. "Hey, girlie, I was thinking about something that just dawned on me. We live in a walkup. You probably aren't going to be able to stay at your place for a while, are you?"

Rayne looked out the window for a moment, trying to collect herself. The last thing she needed was for her friend to see how sad that was making her. She was really starting to get better. She could see herself NOT being here anymore, but she couldn't see herself going anywhere. Her own home wasn't suitable for her at this point, so she had nowhere to go. Eventually she would be able to go home, but not until she could climb three flights of stairs by herself.

She turned back to Sunni after she had gotten her composure a bit and said, "No, not for a while anyway. I can stay here; they won't kick me out if I have nowhere to go. Besides, the trial starts next week, so I can hang out here for a while."

Sunni could tell her friend was trying hard to keep a 'stiff upper lip' as they say, but she saw in her eyes how sad that made Rayne. "Well, I was thinking," she said. "I have a friend that would totally let you stay there. They have a first-floor guest room and the house has a very open plan to it so you could either walk or use the chair if your legs got too tired. They are kind of just banging around all alone in this huge house. I think they might like having a roommate for a while. And I know they would totally respect your privacy." She hesitated to go on, but in for a penny....in for a pound. Here went nothing. "And don't be mad at me, but I kind of ran the idea past them and they are totally open to the idea, just until you are completely back on your feet so to speak. It isn't permanent or anything. But they totally have the space."

Rayne thought about that and couldn't believe anyone would open their home to her. "But why would they do that?"

"It's just a good Samaritan kind of thing, I think. They have the space, you need the first-floor thing, it works out." Sunni did her best to sound nonchalant, like this was really no big deal. *Come on, Rayne, take the bait,* she thought. *You will be so happy if you do.* "Look, I asked if maybe we could drop by this afternoon and I could show you the room. No pressure. Just see if it's something that could work for you short term. Just going to look can't be all that bad, can it?"

Rayne thought about it. She was stronger now; she was able to walk down the hall to get to therapy by herself. She could probably make it into the house. She might have to sit down often, but for some reason this seemed important to Sunni and she didn't want to let her friend down. She wouldn't take the actual room, that wasn't something that she could do, but she could go look. Like Sunni said, it couldn't be all that bad to get out on a gorgeous day and go for a drive. "Okay, I'll go look, but while we are out, I want a milkshake. I never used to get those."

"Okay, tour, then milkshake. Got it!" Sunni said.

They pulled up to a massive home, but Sunni drove to the carport at the side of the house. Rayne looked at her sort of oddly, so she quickly explained, "The front door has a few steps, but there is a side door that goes through the kitchen that is all one level."

"Oh, okay." Rayne did not sound convinced at all.

Sunni got out of the car and walked around to wait for Rayne to join her near the side door. "Let's go look. I think you're going to love this place, if you just give it a chance." She opened the door and Rayne followed her inside. "So, obviously, this is the kitchen and the spare guest room is right through here."

Rayne looked around. The kitchen was massive and yes, very open and spacious. She could use her chair here if she needed to. She was hoping that she wouldn't need to, but it was good to have options. *Wait,* she thought to herself, *what am I thinking? I'm not even really considering staying here.* She followed Sunni to a door and got a brief glimpse of a mammoth living room to her right. When they walked into the bedroom, Rayne had to admit the space was beautiful and again, very open and spacious. She could see herself being comfortable here, but staying with a stranger just wasn't something she could see herself being comfortable with.

"Through that door is the bathroom. Girl, when you see that room you are going to think you died and went to heaven. A jetted tub that you can like totally to submerge yourself in, a separate shower with one of those rain head things. Room to spread out all your makeup and girly stuff. I personally would kill for that bathroom," Sunni said, pointing to the door on the other side of the room.

Rayne walked into the room and, sure enough, Sunni hadn't been lying. This room was a bathroom to die for—again, if she would consider living with a stranger, which she totally wouldn't. But if she would, this would totally be the place to do it. She looked at the tub longingly. Yeah, that would be so amazing on her sore muscles, like the therapy tub at the facility. She allowed herself a few minutes to dream that this really was her bathroom. But she had to stop wasting Sunni's time. This really wasn't something she could do. As she walked out of the bathroom, she started with "Look, Sunni, I appreciate..." but trailed off when she saw Walt standing there. "What are you doing here?" She was really confused now.

"Uh—" He kind of stammered and ran his hands through his hair. She had noticed he did that when he was looking for the right words to say. It did absolutely nothing to take away from his total hotness either. Mussed-up hair looked good on him. "I, uh, I live here."

Rayne's eyes widened and she stammered a little herself. "You...live here." What the hell were Sunni and Walt thinking, and speaking of Sunni, where the hell had she run off to?

Walt noticed her looking around for her friend and so he assured her, "Don't worry, Sunni didn't abandon you. She's out by the pool enjoying some cool lemonade while we talk."

Of course she is, Rayne thought. There was a pool, with cold lemonade. Was there anything that this house didn't have?

"Look, just hear me out here, please. I totally talked Sunni into all of this," Walt pleaded. He moved closer and took her hand in his. "I would really like for you to come here to stay for however long you need to. I know you live next door to Sunni. In a third-floor walkup. You can't go there right now, that's pretty obvious."

She had to give him that one, but that didn't mean she was moving in.

"Anyway, just listen, please. I have a housekeeper who does all the shopping and who makes meals that can be reheated or microwaved. This room would be totally yours, totally as private as you want it to be. I installed an intercom system so that you can get a hold of me or Mrs. Steele when she is here if you ever need anything."

"I really appreciate all that you have done, but really, I can't accept your generosity," Rayne protested.

"Please sit for a moment," Walt said, pointing to a chair in the corner. It was a big comfy chair, the kind you could get lost in a book or even doze off for a while and not feel at all cramped when you woke up. She sat down and he pulled the ottoman over so that they were eye to eye. "The first day I walked into your room at that rehab facility, all I could think was how dull and drab it was. To be honest with you, Rayne, I'm not doing this for you, I'm doing it for me." She started to protest, but he held up his hand. "Just let me finish, please." She nodded and he went on. "Rayne, you are the most beautiful woman I have ever met, both inside and outside. I know that you have survived a tragedy, but that just makes you more beautiful because you survived it. When I first met you, I could tell that you were so hurt, not just physically. But in the last few weeks, you have made so much progress. But you are too beautiful to sit in that rehab facility, surrounded by all that dullness. I don't know exactly where things will go between you and me, I hope they continue, because I really care about you. But this is not contingent on that; there is no pressure to do anything with me. I promise I won't take advantage of you while you are here. I just want you to be in a place where you can be comfortable and heal. Bring anything you need or want to from home. If there is something that will help you get better that I don't have, I'll get it. But, please, Rayne, for me, use my home for the rest of your healing process. We can hire therapists to come here, or you can go to the facility for sessions, which ever feels best to you. I have a pool, an exercise room, a tub you can relax in after a hard day of therapy. Whatever you need, sweetheart. I'll get it for you, but please let me take you out of that dull lifeless place." Walt was pleading now, he knew he was. He could argue with the best of them in court, but he really hoped he was making his case with this beautiful petite woman. Somehow, this mattered more than any court case he had ever been assigned.

Rayne had tears streaming down her face by the time he was done. "Um, that was quite the speech." She said. Walt just gave her a sort of shrug and a half smile like he wasn't going to back down or apologize for anything he had said. "I just have a couple of questions. First, why would you do this for me?" she asked.

"Well, like I said, you're beautiful and I care about you," Walt said softly.

Rayne looked deep into his eyes. What she saw there was the honesty of the words he had spoken. "Okay, next thing. I don't have a lot, but I really want to pay you some sort of room and board," she said firmly. Walt started shaking his head adamantly, but she persisted. "Walt, I insist."

"No, Rayne." He took both of her hands in his. "Listen to me. I am your attorney; I know what your situation is. When we win this case, we can talk about whether you owe me any rent. Besides, as your attorney, this saves me so much time in travel to the facility, and I know for certain you will make it to court every day." He smiled and winked at her. "But seriously though, Rayne, if this goes the way I am hoping it may, there is no way I could accept rent from my girlfriend." She liked the sound of that part. "But I will ask one favor in return," he said.

"What's that?" she asked softly.

"Spend time with me, eat meals with me. This house is so big and so quiet, it will be nice to have someone to share meals with and watch shows with or whatever. And, like I said, when you are physically able to go back to your apartment, I will accept your decision if you leave."

Rayne took a deep breath. Could this really be happening? This man, this gorgeous, amazing man, the one that any woman would feel lucky to be with, was asking her to spend time with him. Was offering her a beautiful place to stay that fit all her physical limitations. He cared about her; she could see it in his eyes. He really did care. She would be a fool to say no to this and to not at least take a shot to see where this might go. Finally, she looked back up at him and said, "Okay, but I have one request of my own." Walt looked like he wasn't quite prepared for what her request was going to be, but he would hear her out. "Can we dance together sometimes too?" she asked shyly.

Walt stood up and lifted her off the chair, wrapped his arms around her, and with the biggest smile she had ever seen he said, "Yeah, sweetheart, we can dance, we can dance under the stars, we can dance on the rooftop, we can dance every day if that's what you want."

Rayne was sort of breathless with the excitement of being swung around and the excitement that was clearly coming from Walt. She didn't know how they would dance on rooftops, but it all sounded good to her. Walt leaned down and took her mouth with his for a long, slow kiss. When he finished, he told her, "You've made me very happy, sweetheart. Very happy."

He started to carry her out of the room, and she tried to struggle against him. "Where are you taking me?" she protested.

"We have to go tell Sunni the good news," he said, smiling down at her. She gave up the fight and let him carry her outside. Yep, she was falling head over heels for this guy. She had never really known what love felt like before, but she was pretty sure this was it.

****

After they shared the news with Sunni, she suggested they all go out for that milkshake that Rayne had asked for. Over greasy burgers, onion rings, French fries and milkshakes, they decided to move Rayne's things the following day. "There really isn't much to move, just my toiletries and clothes," she stated.

"But aren't there things that you want from your apartment? See, Rayne, that's what I am hoping to change. That room is so bare, so not you. There is nothing of you in it. I want you to feel like my place is your home for however long you may need it. I want you to bring your pictures and your knick-knacks, whatever makes it feel more like home for you," Walt replied.

"Those things will have to wait. There is no way I can go and get them right now."

"Ah, but haven't you heard the old saying, 'where there's a will there's a way'? Trust me, we will get anything you want from home."

"You aren't going to carry me up three flights of stairs just so that I can get a few things," she protested. She had turned her head down, like she was shy about all of this.

"I will if that's what it takes, or I can support you while you walk or, whatever." Walt leaned forward and put a finger under her chin and tilted her eyes back up so they met his. "It's not like you weigh much, sweetheart. I can carry you or help you in anyway necessary. Okay?"

She simply nodded. What could she say? She had a lump the size of Texas in her throat. Oh, this man and what he could do to her with a simple touch or a simple word.

"Well, now that that part is settled, I know where I can get some boxes, so what time are we meeting tomorrow?" Sunni asked to help lighten things. She had a feeling Rayne was about to cry again over the things that Walt was willing to do for her. What her friend didn't realize was that Walt had probably been in love with Rayne for a few weeks now.

Chapter Eleven

By 9:00 a.m. when Walt and Sunni arrived, Rayne already had all her things stacked on the bed. A nurse had come in and helped her strip the bed and get her things around. She really didn't have much to pack. All she had here were some sweats and yoga pants, T-shirts and tank tops and of course her underthings. She had the basic toiletries and of course, she had her sloth. She smiled when she remembered Walt giving it to her. He had seemed almost nervous about giving her the silly thing, like he wasn't sure if she would take it or not. Little did he know that it had meant so much to her to have him give it to her. It would always hold a special place in her heart.

When Walt got out of his car, Sunni was standing near the door of the facility waiting for him. When he reached her, she stopped him and said, "Look, I just want to say thanks again for all that you are doing for Rayne. I don't know if she has said it or not, but this really means a lot to her, and therefore, it really means a lot to me too."

"It's no big deal," Walt protested.

"But it is a big deal, and it really means a lot, to both of us." Sunni smiled.

Walt felt kind of awkward, but he opened the door and let Sunni precede him inside.

When they had everything in boxes, Sunni suddenly said, "Oh, wait shouldn't we go outside and get the wind...." She stopped right there, but realized that it was already too late; the cat was out of the bag, so to speak. If Rayne hadn't known where the wind chimes came from before, she most certainly did now. At least she knew someone had put it there. She might not be sure which of them had done it, though.

"Wait, why would we take the wind chimes? It was put there a while ago. I think maybe the person in the next room..." She looked from Sunni to Walt and back again, neither one seemed to be interested in meeting her eyes directly. "Unless it is mine and was put there for me.... Okay, which one of you did it?"

Walt slowly raised his hand, still not meeting her eyes. He seemed like maybe he wasn't sure if she would be okay with that. But she totally was. At first, she had thought it was odd that someone had put it there, but she had shrugged it off, assuming the person in the next room had a family member that had put it there for them to enjoy. She had woken every morning to the wonder of rainbows bouncing off the walls and surfaces of her room. It had made the mornings more cheerful. But it had been there for weeks. Like days after she had met him. She had no doubt that it had been Sunni that had told him she liked rainbows. Hence the guilty looks on both of their faces.

"Guys, hey, did you think I would be upset that it got put there? Because I'm not." Turning to Sunni, she said, "I assume it was you that told him I love rainbows." Sunni nodded, and, turning to Walt, she continued, "and it was you who got it and put it up out there."

"Well, no. Technically," Walt said, "it was Zak that actually put it up, but yes, I am the one who got it."

These two, they obviously cared for her so much, it made her eyes water. Since her parents had died, she had put so much into trying to be the best dancer she could that she hadn't really taken time to build relationships with anyone. She and Sunni had basically known each other forever. They had met in elementary school and had become fast and forever friends. But with all the hours she had put into dancing, she rarely had time to go out and socialize and make new friends. She had girls in dance classes that she was friendly with, but none that she really considered a friend. And, wasn't the fact that none of them had even come to visit, either in the hospital, nor at the rehabilitation facility telling of just how they felt? No, they weren't really friends, they were just people who talked and spent time together because they were working on a similar goal. These two people were the only ones in her life that really cared about her.

She needed to be careful, though. She wanted more with Walt, and he seemed to want more too, but the last thing she needed was to push him away by needing him too much. She kind of wanted to leave the wind chime there so that maybe it would brighten the days of the next person who stayed in this room, but she didn't want to hurt Walt's feelings by seeming to reject his gift. Finally, she stammered, "Well, um, then thank you, both of you for your thoughtfulness and kindness. I really appreciate it. Um, I was wondering though, if it's all right with you, Walt, maybe we could just leave it there." She rushed on before he got the wrong impression. "It's not that I don't love it, I do, but that tree and that wind chime is in the perfect place to catch the morning sun and it brightens this room so much. I was thinking maybe it might be a nice thing for whoever gets this room next." By the time she was finished, she was looking down at the floor, not wanting to see it if there was a look or hurt on Walt's face.

Walt walked over to Rayne and put his finger under her chin to lift her eyes to his. It seemed like he was doing that a lot lately. One day his girl would be more confident and not try to hide when she was afraid that he wouldn't like her answer. "I think it's a wonderful idea," Walt agreed. "And if you really like it, we can always get more."

Rayne wasn't sure how much money Walt made. From his home and car, it seemed like maybe it was an awful lot, but still, she wasn't taking advantage of him or his money. "Oh, well, for now, let's not worry about getting another one. You have done so much for me already," she said.

And I want to do so much more, Walt thought to himself. Well, she could say she didn't want him to do all the things she wanted, but he could and would do whatever he thought might make her happy. He understood how she felt. She probably hadn't had many people do a lot for her in life, especially after her parents had died. And he knew she had never had a boyfriend who bought things for her or who treated her as special. So he was just going to have to show her what it was like to have a boyfriend that really cared. And, whether she admitted it or not, they both knew that was exactly what they were, boyfriend and girlfriend. It might seem kind of odd, him being 27 and feeling like a kid with his new girlfriend, but he also knew that Rayne was less experienced than he was and so he would take it as slow as she needed him to. Besides, it wasn't totally ethical to sleep with a client. So, until her case was over, he had to walk a very careful line to help her but also remain professional.

"Okay, so we leave the wind chime for the next resident of this room. Onward to your apartment to get the rest of your things," Walt said.

"Oh, um, no, that's fine. I don't need to go there. Besides, I can't exactly climb up the stairs to work on packing," Rayne objected. She was getting much better at walking short distances without needing to rest, but there was no way she was going to be able to climb three flights of stairs. "The things there can wait until I am up to the climb or until I am ready to move back home."

That was the whole point: Walt didn't want her to ever move back home. He was pretty sure he was really going to like having her around so much that he wouldn't want her to leave. The more of her things that were at his place, the harder it would be for her to just leave and go back home. "Look, sweetheart, I really want you to have your personal things, your photos and books or whatever else it is that you might need to make my place feel more like your home. I really want you to feel like it's your home for however long you need it, so, please, let me help you get the things from your apartment."

"Okay, if it means that much to you, we can go. If you will help me, I can climb them. You don't need to carry me," she stated in a way that said she didn't want any argument.

By the time Rayne made it all the way up the steps, with a huge amount of support from the handrails and Walt, she was exhausted. Sunni suggested that she just sit and point at things in the living room and kitchen area for Walt to pack while Sunni went and worked on the things she was sure Rayne would want from the bathroom and bedroom. The packing proceeded rather quickly that way. Before leaving, Rayne double-checked the rooms Sunni had done but her friend hadn't missed a thing. They separated the boxes efficiently and labeled everything so that Rayne would only have to unpack the boxes as she wanted or needed to.

Walt boxed her personal photos and things from the living room area. Every time he picked one up, Rayne would tell him who they were. Mostly it was photos of her with a parent at some dance event where she always wore ribbons or medals for her achievements. Some were still shots of her during a performance. There were several photos of Rayne and Sunni out doing things, making funny faces at the camera, or laughing with each other. Walt packed them with special care. He realized that he wanted those photos placed around his home, not just in the room that she was going to be staying in. He wanted to intermingle them with his photos. In his mind, he compared them to the photos he had of his family. There weren't a lot of them to be found. Most of the ones he did have were formal family photos. He had a few photos of him and his former frat brothers/current brewery co-owners. Hers seemed to have more life in them than most of his did, though. He wanted them to become a part of their home. He knew he had only offered for her to stay until she could move back into her apartment with more ease, but he found himself wanting to make her more and more a part of his life and his home.

By the time they had the few boxes packed up, Rayne found herself starting to drift off. She hadn't had this much physical activity in a few months, and this was wearing on her hard. She didn't protest at all when Walt told her to stay put until he had the boxes packed in his SUV and then he would be back for her. She didn't even protest when Walt picked her up and started carrying her down the stairs. She just put her head on his shoulder and drifted back off to sleep. Walt tucked her into the passenger seat of his SUV and buckled her in tightly. There was a certain amount of satisfaction in that whole encounter. She obviously trusted him; she could rely on him to keep her safe and take care of her. It gave her a warm and happy feeling knowing that those things were true.

Walt spent the drive back to his place in deep thought. He wasn't sure exactly what was going on in his head. He had always been pretty much a playboy, like all his buddies. He didn't use women; they always knew the score, it was all just fun. He had also always been a pretty dominant person in life, but most especially when it came to sex and relationships. Yet, with Rayne, he had such tender thoughts for her so many times. It was most likely because of what she had been through. He hadn't wanted to go in with his usual brashness when he knew how much she had been hurt in the last year. But there was a part of him, that dominant part, that really wanted to protect her and make sure she didn't get hurt again. If he were to be totally honest with himself, yes, there was a part of him that wondered what she would look like tied spread eagle to his bed, or how her ass would look with his handprint on it, but those were things that would have to wait. There was a line that he should not cross when it came to impropriety with a client. No matter how much he wanted her, that would all have to wait until her case was over, if she would even be interested in such things. He didn't know. She was obviously a virgin—hell, she'd said she hadn't ever really been kissed before him. Maybe this whole attraction thing of his would turn out to be a bad idea. But, bad idea or not, ability to have sex with her or not, the right to dominate her or not, he could not help but want to keep her safe and make her life easier by not having to stay in that walkup apartment. He would just have to do his best to keep his distance for the time being. Fortunately for him, the trial started Monday and while it would likely be somewhat lengthy because both sides would be calling in expert after expert to try to prove their viewpoint, there was at least an end somewhere in sight.

Walt carried her into her room and laid her gently on the bed. She woke and sat up and started to stand. "No, sweetheart, you are wiped out, don't try to get up. Just tell me what you need, and I'll get it for you," Walt stated.

"Well, I need to change into some pajamas, so I will need the suitcase we packed at the facility, and something to drink would be helpful. Maybe a glass of water or tea," she replied.

"I can manage that. I don't have tea now, but I will bring your suitcase in and some water, okay? You just try to relax. We have a big day ahead of us tomorrow." He brushed some hair away from her face and kissed her forehead gently before leaving the room.

Walt made his way to the kitchen and grabbed a bottle of water from the fridge. He also pulled out the pad of paper where he wrote notes to his housekeeper and asked her to pick up a variety of teas when she did the shopping. Smiling to himself, he went out to the garage and grabbed the suitcase and a box. He would have a couple of trips to get it all in the house, but he wanted her to have the suitcase and her photos first. Nothing would make her feel more like this was her space than having her own photos and mementos here—at least he hoped that was the case. When he entered the room, Rayne was sitting up in the big easy chair in the corner, obviously trying to stay awake until her clothing arrived for her to change. He put the suitcase on the bed to make it easier for her to get things out of it and then sat the box near the door. "I brought in the box of photos and things. I thought maybe you would want some of them to make the room feel more 'yours,'" Walt stated. "Why don't you go ahead and get what you need out of the suitcase for tonight, and I'll set it back on the floor for you. I don't want you having to lift it. I am sure we can get it all unpacked tomorrow."

"Okay, but, really, I'm not an invalid, I'm just really tired. I think I overdid it today," she admitted.

He smiled at her. "I know you're not an invalid. You are capable of so much more than even you realize, I think. But if you are up for it, I think maybe we should talk a little bit about tomorrow before you go to bed. You go ahead and get changed and I'll go get a couple more boxes."

"Okay." She stood and rummaged through the suitcase, finding a sleep set and her toiletries and headed for the bathroom.

Walt removed the suitcase from the bed and used his pocketknife to open the box of photos in case she wanted to put any of them up before she settled in for the night. Then he proceeded to head to the garage for a few more boxes. She really didn't have much stuff, mostly clothing and her mementos. She had a makeup case and a few other small items. She really hadn't needed to bring a lot. His home was fully stocked with anything she could want other than her personal items and tea, Walt reminded himself. He didn't have tea. Hopefully Mrs. Steele would rectify that tomorrow. When Walt knocked on her door, he heard her softly say "come in" before he proceeded inside. She was wearing a pair of yoga pants and a tank top. She really looked sexy dressed like that. Walt didn't know what made him feel like that look was sexy, but there was something about it that just did it for him. She sat on the bed, massaging her injured leg. Walt thought about offering to help her with that, but he knew that the more he put his hands on her, the harder it would be for him to keep their relationship professional. Instead he set down the things he was carrying and sat in the big stuffed chair across from her bed.

"So I just wanted to kind of give you a heads up on what will happen tomorrow in court. It's just opening arguments, so really, there isn't anything that you will have to do other than be there and be yourself," Walt began. "I will have an opportunity to explain to the judge and the jury why I believe the construction company was negligent and why we feel that they should have to pay out a settlement. Their attorney will basically say why they don't believe they are in the wrong or why they don't feel that they owe you any money. It's nothing for you to worry about. They may come across like they are trying to say you are lying or that you are doing this to try to get rich off the construction company, but that's just the way they must start. If they had been willing to accept responsibility for what happened, they would have offered a settlement before now. For whatever reason, they are choosing to try to fight this. And so it will become my job over the rest of the trial to prove that they are at fault." He looked at her, hoping that she could see that he really had very little worry that they would win the case. "Do you have any questions?"

"Not so much about tomorrow. You've explained that fairly well. But what else will I be facing the rest of the time, as things proceed?" Rayne asked.

"Well, first of all, I want you to know that I will be beside you every step of the way, and not just as your attorney, but as someone who cares about you too." He gave her what he hoped was an encouraging smile. "Each evening, we will sit down over dinner and discuss what happened that day and what I expect will be happening the next day. We will also go over your statement and the answers to the questions their attorney will most likely ask you." Walt paused for a moment, realizing that there was something else he should probably cover with her. "Speaking of questions, there will likely be reporters outside the courthouse. For tomorrow, just keep your head down and allow me to shelter you from them. Let me do any talking that may need to be done. As we progress, we can discuss if there is a time that you should make a statement or answer questions of the press, but for tomorrow, don't worry about that at all. Okay?"

She looked at him like a frightened mouse and said "Okay" so softly he almost wasn't sure she had said it at all.

Walt walked over and sat beside her on the bed and put an arm around her. "It will be all right, Rayne. I promise you it will be okay. Just trust me to do my job." She slowly nodded against his chest. There wasn't any more he could do to reassure her at this point. He just needed to go in there and kick ass and take names like a boss so she could see that she had nothing to worry about. He kissed her on the top of the head again and stood to leave the room. He turned back and told her, "I hope you feel like you can make yourself at home here for however long you stay. Feel free to unpack and put things wherever you feel like they would look best."

"Thank you," she said, smiling at him. She looked so tired as she added, "for everything."

"It's my pleasure. Now, get some sleep. We should leave by 9:00 in the morning. Do you need me to wake you up or do you have an alarm?" he asked.

"I have one on my phone that I will set. Good night, Walt."

"Good night, Rayne." He gently closed her door and walked to the stairs that would take him to the master suite upstairs. Suddenly, his big king size bed seemed like a very lonely place to be.

Chapter Twelve

At 8:00 a.m., Rayne made her way from her room out to the kitchen to find Walt standing there in dress slacks and a button-down dress shirt facing the coffee maker. His suit coat and tie were over the back of one of the stools at the breakfast bar that separated the kitchen from the dining room. He had two place mats set on the table with silverware and glasses. When he noticed her out of the corner of his eye, he tuned to her and asked if she wanted any coffee. She nodded so he poured her a cup. On the table, she noticed cream and sugar were already set waiting for her. It seemed that Walt was a host who thought of everything.

"I wasn't sure what you might want to do about breakfast," he said, running a hand through his hair like he was sort of thrown off by not knowing what to have for her or what she might want. "Mrs. Steele always leaves things that I can make an easy omelet out of and there is always fresh fruit. Orange juice, milk, cereal. Just let me know what you want."

She felt bad asking him to cook for her, so she hesitated.

"I was going to make a spinach and white cheddar omelet for myself," Walt offered. He kind of sensed that she wouldn't have asked for it herself, but when he added, "It would be just as easy to make two if that sounds good to you," he could see her face brighten a bit.

"That sounds delicious," she said as her stomach growled loudly. Her face immediately got hot and she was sure red.

"It sounds like I better get to cooking then," Walt teased.

"It's just that with all the moving yesterday, I probably didn't eat as much as I should have, but this will put things back right with my metabolism," she said.

Walt began scrambling the eggs for the omelet. "There's juice or milk in the fridge if you would like either."

She opened the door and decided on orange juice for herself.

"Would you like anything while I am here?" she asked.

"Sure, sweetheart, I wouldn't mind some orange juice."

She took the container and poured them each a glass at the table. She took it back to the fridge and turned to see if she could offer him any other assistance, but instead he said to her, "You should go sit. I don't want you overworked today, this is going to be a long day for you."

She liked that he was concerned, but she didn't want to feel like a burden either. She went and sat at the table as she was told.

When Walt brought the plates to the table, he noticed that she was just sitting there silently. He hoped she wasn't too nervous about court today. Of all the days she would attend, today was probably one of the easiest, other than hearing the details of her accident all over again. Maybe that was what had her seeming to be withdrawn and quiet. "So are you worried about today?" he asked.

"No, not really. I trust that you know what you are doing," she said while cutting at her omelet.

"Okay. It's just that you seem rather quiet suddenly. I was hoping it wasn't the court case that was bothering you."

"No, I just—" She picked at her food a bit, then added quietly, "I just don't want to feel like a burden to you or anyone. I know I can't do a lot of standing or walking yet, but I do want to help with whatever I can."

Walt put his finger under her chin and gently lifted her face to look at him. "I'm sorry, sweetheart. I tend to be a dominant overbearing ass sometimes. I just want to keep you from causing yourself pain. But I do realize that you can do a lot more than I probably want you to. I'm overprotective that way, but point taken. You can help more in the future, I promise." He brushed his thumb along her jawline and looked into her eyes. "Okay, and, if I get to be too overbearing, feel free to call me on it."

"Okay." She smiled at him and when he withdrew his hand she dug into her omelet with renewed strength. She knew she wasn't all better and that she still had a way to go on her therapy, but she felt like she needed to 'begin as she planned to go,' as they say. If she came off as a total mooch, Walt wouldn't want her around for long. She felt like she needed to establish a pattern of helping with what she could and pushing herself to do more as she could.

As they began eating, Walt said, "About today, I want to let you know what to expect. Basically, no one needs to prove that you were injured; the medical facts take care of that. However, it's my job to prove that A. The injury was caused by the accident that was caused by the construction company and that B. Those injuries affected not only your current health, but also have lasting effects into the future."

"Okay" she said softly. Walt could tell that she was thinking about all that she had lost due to the injury.

"Now, on the other hand," he began again, "what they are going to try to do is prove two things. They are going to try to say that your injuries aren't really affecting you as much as we say they are and that they aren't at fault for the injury in the first place."

Rayne looked at him with big eyes and started to protest. If they could convince the judge or jury that they weren't at fault, she would lose everything.

"Wait a minute, let me finish," Walt implored. "Like I said, medical proof says that your injuries are what we say they are. They will have an 'expert'"—he used the finger air quotes around the word—"that will say that your injuries are not as severe as we say they are, or who will try to say that they are what we say they are, but that they don't affect your ability to have a normal future. Trust me, I have experts and exhibits that will show that we are right on this one." He looked at her and she gave a small nod as if to say she would have to take his word for it for now. So Walt continued, "The other thing they are going to try to argue is where things become more complex. They may argue that their employee did everything right, that it must be the equipment that was faulty. Therefore, they will say we should be suing the company that made the bands that were used to secure the pipes. Or they may try to claim that the road itself had a pothole or other defect that caused the truck to shift in a way that was abnormal for the anchoring system. Therefore, we should be suing the city that maintains the roads. Those are just a couple of the scenarios that I have seen attorneys try in the past. Really, the possibilities are endless. They will try to point the blame at anyone but themselves. It's how the system works."

He looked at her and waited till she was making full eye contact. "After all, if they walked in and accepted responsibility, there would be no reason to argue the case and my job would be done." He noticed a brief flash of something in her eyes. Was that maybe a little panic that when the case was over, they would be done? He could assure her that wouldn't be the case, but for now, he had to keep things as professional as possible and hoping that she was falling for him as much as he was falling for her had to wait until the business side of this was over.

When they were both finished, she cleared the table. As she walked to the kitchen, Walt said, "Just put them in the dishwasher. Mrs. Steele will be here later, and she will be dirtying dishes to prepare meals for the next few days. She will run the dishwasher before she leaves, and we can empty it later. We can do it together so that you see where things go."

Rayne smiled. Maybe he could learn to let her help in some small ways at least. She went back to her room to finish preparing for the day in court. At least as much as she could prepare anyway. At ten minutes before 9:00 she was ready and waiting at the kitchen table. Walt came into the room a minute later. He had gone somewhere and put on his tie. Most likely tying it in a mirror. When he put on his suit coat, he looked like the devastatingly handsome man that had walked into her room at the facility that first day. He was kind of devastatingly handsome in pretty much anything, as far as she could tell. They both headed out to his garage. Inside, he had both the sports car he had driven her home in the night of their first "date" as Rayne liked to think of it and the SUV they had used yesterday for moving her things.

"You have two cars, and it's just you?" she asked.

"Yeah, I like the car for most things, but the SUV sometimes comes in handy with having the brewery. Sometimes it's easier to pick up a load of napkins or whatever than it is to have to wait for them to ship," he said as he expertly maneuvered the vehicle out of the garage and down his long driveway. "Do you drive?"

"I know how to. I just don't have a car because I live on the bus routes and pretty much everywhere I go is on the route. Sometimes, Sunni takes me places if I need to. It was just cheaper to not have a car. Dancing doesn't pay very well in towns like this," she added as she looked out the window.

That was something that Walt had never really thought about. She probably hadn't had much money. Maybe she had some inheritance from her parents, but most likely that wasn't a lot. Especially if the apartment and lack of car was any indication. "Well, you are welcome to use mine if you need it for anything. Just ask. I know I kind of live out of the city and off the beaten path, so to speak," Walt offered.

"Thanks. I'm not really sure I am up to driving yet but thank you for the offer," Rayne said. She couldn't imagine driving this sporty little car and she couldn't imagine driving his big monstrosity of an SUV. She would just stay in or maybe she could still get Sunni to take her places occasionally. Her therapist was set up to come to Walt's house, and he'd said his housekeeper did all the grocery shopping, so she really wouldn't need to go out much.

As he slowed down approaching the courthouse, Walt saw the reporters in a mob outside of the building. He had already called his admin that morning and told her that due to the sensitive nature of this case, he would be using one of the parking spaces his firm kept rented in the underground garage beside the courthouse. If any of the more senior partners had an issue with it, they could call him. He was glad he had done so when Rayne started to noticeably stiffen and fidget when she saw the mob. "It's okay, we will go in through the side entrance," Walt assured her. "Our law firm keeps a few parking spaces in this underground garage right here." He turned to pull into the garage and took a left toward the area marked with the name of the firm. The sign on the wall designated the spaces as belonging to Owens, Jensen, Hallowell and Stein. Yep, being the son of one of the founding partners sometimes had its perks.

Rayne reached for her door handle just as Walt put out a hand to stop her. "Let me open your door for you, Rayne." When she looked at him questioningly, he shrugged his shoulders. "Overbearing, dominant asshole, remember?" he said then gave her his amazing smile. She dropped her hand and waited for him to open her door and take her hand to help her out of the vehicle. After reaching in the back seat for his briefcase, he placed a hand at the small of her back and directed her to the side entrance of the building. They went through the metal detectors and made their way to the elevators. The elevator was crowded at this time of day. Most courts where just getting ready to start. When they stepped off the elevator, he put his hand back at her lower back. He told himself he was doing it to guide her in the right direction of their room and add a reassurance that things would be okay. Walt introduced Rayne to his paralegal. Normally by this point in the case, the paralegal would have been in contact with Rayne on a regular basis, but this case was different for him. He was doing the client contact himself. His paralegal probably found that odd, but oh well.

He leaned over just before the judge entered and said quietly in her ear, "Just remember, this will most likely be painful in a lot of ways. You will see and hear things that I am sure you would rather forget, but trust me, it's necessary and I'm doing it for you." Just as he finished, a door opened, the judge started to walk into the room and the bailiff let out a commanding "All rise." Rayne stood with everyone else and waited for the judge to tell them to be seated. As she sat in her seat, she felt a hand touch her shoulder from behind and turned to see Sunni's reassuring smile. At least she had one friendly face—well, one besides Walt. She didn't know what she would do if she didn't have Walt and Sunni on her side.

By the end of the day, the entire situation had lived up to exactly what Walt said it would be. He gave a statement of why they were suing, what he intended to prove and what damages they were seeking. He was suing for 25 million dollars. He had told her that they most likely wouldn't get that, and maybe not even come close to that, but he was going to try to argue for lost wages as well as pain and suffering. As he also asked the judge and jury, what price tag did you put on someone's lifelong dream? Rayne found herself thinking about the whole situation. There was a time when she'd felt like no amount of money would be good enough; she just wanted someone to pay. And although she wasn't in that same totally depressed place anymore, the truth was that she would need to support herself somehow, but she knew she could get some form of job. And, today, there wasn't any other way to make someone pay for the damage that had been done to her other than to give her a monetary award. They hadn't done anything illegal, so there were no legal charges to be brought. All they could do was try to make the person do penance by having to pay money.

Walt had been exactly right about what he'd said about the construction company attorney. It wasn't their fault....it must have been faulty equipment.... yes, there was physical damage, but was there as much as she claimed.... etc., etc., etc. For the most part, Rayne found that she had to tune the attorney out or she was going to be rolling her eyes and shaking her head at just how much they were trying to avoid taking any responsibility at all.

When both attorneys had finished with their opening statements, the judge retired the case for the day. They would be back tomorrow morning and Walt would start making his case with documents and experts and whatever else he felt he needed to use to prove his case. Rayne wasn't sure that she wanted to see and hear all the details of her life all over again. She had lived it; she didn't want to see it all paraded around for everyone to see and hear. However, she also knew that she had to be there; she had to be 'real' to these people. Walt had explained to her that they would be much more sympathetic to a young woman sitting there fighting her case when they could see the pain in her eyes. As much as it sucked to be watched like that, she knew it had to be done.

When they got back to Walt's house, it was time for her therapist to show up. Walt excused himself to go change into something more comfortable and said he would be in his home office working on the case. He told Rayne to buzz him on the intercom system when her therapy was done, and they would decide what to do for dinner.

Rayne was tired from her weekend move and the draining day in court. She apologized to Keeley for her lack of enthusiasm and effort. But Keeley shook it off. "You've come so far, Rayne. So much progress since you left the facility even. You don't have to apologize for one bad day." She helped Rayne sit in the chair on the back deck. They had decided to do much of her therapy outside for however long the weather would allow. "Tell you what, I don't see you again until Wednesday. If you get a chance, maybe try to swim a few laps in that gorgeous pool back there between now and then. That will make up for today's session." She held out her hand and asked, "Deal?"

Rayne shook her hand with a smile and said, "Deal," She would find time to get into the pool and, maybe, she could convince Walt to dance with her after dinner. That would give her some exercise too.

Rayne went inside and changed back out of her workout clothes into something she hoped was flattering. She had never really paid a lot of attention to clothing. She was either in dance clothes or costumes for performances and when she was at home, it was sweats or yoga pants. She only had a few outfits that she considered 'safe for public consumption.' Hopefully she was dressed okay for her first real evening in Walt's house. Last night hadn't counted since she was asleep before her head hit the pillow practically. She buzzed the intercom to let Walt know she was ready to prepare dinner or whatever whenever he was. He told her he would be right down. She met him a few minutes later in the kitchen.

"You don't know how glad I am to have someone here to share my evening with," he said, smiling. "There is always more food than one person can eat in the meals my housekeeper makes, so I end up having each of them more than one time." He walked to the fridge and opened the door. "Let's see what our choices are," he said. Walt listed off several different options for dinner. When he mentioned macaroni and cheese, Rayne's eyes lit up. Walt didn't miss the change in her facial expression. "Mac and cheese, it is then." He pulled a baking dish out of the refrigerator.

"We don't have to, if you would prefer something else," Rayne said. "I just realized that I haven't had mac and cheese in ages. Carbs like that aren't great for a dancer's body."

"It's fine, sweetheart, I love it too. That's why Mrs. Steele makes it pretty much every week. It's usually the first thing to go," he said, smiling. He set the oven to heat up and then turned to Rayne. "So, since we are being horribly bad with the carbs, would you like a salad to go with it to balance it out?"

"Sure, that sounds great!" Rayne said enthusiastically.

Walt went to the other side of the breakfast bar and grabbed a stool. He set it in front of the butcher block in the center of the kitchen. "Sit," he told her. "I'll get the stuff and you can help me chop."

Rayne perched herself on the stool and watched as Walt bent over to get the vegetables from the bottom drawer in the fridge. That man did have one fine looking backside. She was still sort of staring when Walt turned around. He caught her staring at him, only now, since he had turned it wasn't his ass she was looking at, but his crotch. She quickly averted her eyes to look up and see a sexy smile teasing across his face. Fortunately, he didn't say anything; he just handed her some carrots and celery and a knife. He stood beside her at the butcher block and while he tore off pieces of lettuce, she sliced and chopped the vegetables. It was all very domestic and something that Rayne could find herself really enjoying long term. She wasn't sure if Walt felt the same way, though, so she just kept chopping like the dutiful guest that she was.

They enjoyed the salad while waiting for the mac and cheese to heat through. When it was done, Walt moved the hot dish to the table. He grabbed plates and glasses while Rayne grabbed the silverware. They made a great team, Walt thought to himself. He could get used to sharing a kitchen and a meal with someone like Rayne. Oh, who was he kidding? He could get used to sharing it with Rayne, not just someone 'like' her. He was falling in deeper and deeper, but he knew he had to keep vigilant. Nothing more than dancing and brief hugs or a peck on the cheek could happen before her case was done. And, depending on how dirty the construction company wanted to play, that could take a while.

After dinner, they cleared the table together. Walt positioned her stool by the silverware drawer and opened the dishwasher. He took out the silverware basket and handed it to her. She began sorting things and putting them away. Conveniently, the other cooking utensils were mostly in the next drawer over so Rayne could put things away while sitting and Walt put the dishes and glasses and things in the cupboards. She watched where things went so she could be more help in the future.

"Honestly," she began, "I don't have to sit, I could help with more than just the silverware."

"Ah, yes, but then you would be on your feet and I might not get a chance to dance with you after we're done," Walt said, his eyebrows going up and down in a teasing motion.

Wow, he wanted to dance with her after dinner. Did life get any better? When they were finished with putting dishes away and the dishes from this evening's dinner were put in the dishwasher, Walt offered Rayne a glass of wine. She accepted. After pouring the wine, he held out her glass and then held out his hand so she could put her hand in his. There was that zip of electricity again. She got down off the stool and Walt led her into the living room. He pushed the coffee table up against the sofa and pushed a few other pieces back, making a nice little area perfect for two people to dance. He placed his iPhone in the docking station and music started coming from the speakers. He took the wine glass from her hand and put in on the shelf near the stereo. Walt pulled her close to him and began to sway to the music. He wasn't the best dancer in the world, but she didn't care. He was dancing with her and that was all that mattered. He never kissed her, which was disappointing, but she understood he was being professional. But he did hold her close through a couple of songs before he said he didn't want to tire her out too much. They sat on the couch with their glasses of wine and discussed what would happen tomorrow in court.

"I'll be honest," Walt said. "The next few days won't be easy on you, but it's what I have to do if we want a chance at winning this case. I must bring out a lot of information that won't be easy to hear. I also need to show them who you are, how you danced before the accident. I'm not going to lie; I will have to talk about a lot of things that I am sure you would rather not hear." He wasn't looking her in the face; he couldn't quite meet her eyes. She could tell that this part wasn't going to be easy for him either.

Rayne ducked her head so that they made eye contact. "I understand, and thank you for warning me. I'll do my best to keep myself in check."

"No, sweetheart, no." He looked at her with real purpose now. "That's not what I was saying. You do not have to try to hold anything in. You be who and what you are. I just wanted you to know that it's not going to be easy. And as much as I can be, I'm here for you. I also texted Sunni to let her know what the next few days will be like. I'm sure she will be more than happy to support you through this."

Wow, she couldn't ask for a better attorney, she couldn't ask for a better man. They spent the next couple of hours enjoying their wine and talking about mundane things for the most part. Just getting to know each other a little better and staying away from the lawsuit and other heavy topics. There would be time for all that later.

Chapter Thirteen

The next couple of days were exactly how Walt had told her they would be. He showed videos and photos of her dancing and with her awards and medals. He had her doctor talk about just exactly what had happened to her physically and what her prognosis was. He had stated that she would regain most of her ability to walk although with a slight limp, but no, she would not ever be able to dance in the capacity that she had before. He had an expert who talked about what her future could have been like if she had continued the path toward being a prima ballerina. He had her therapist talk about her progress, but also about her limitations. It was excruciatingly painful. Sunni sat directly behind her and placed her hand on Rayne's shoulder frequently. Walt looked at her numerous times to offer his strength, even though he was walking around the room. Whenever he had to come back to the table to pick up an exhibit or go through his notes, he paused and met her eyes. She knew that he had to be careful in the courtroom, but he did everything he could to let her know that he was there for her and that if he could save her any of this pain, he would.

Tuesday evening, Walt suggested that they simply pick up a pizza on the way home. It had been an exhausting day and he said it might be easier than having to try to figure out what to cook when they got home. They picked up the pizza and ate it in front of the television with a glass of wine.

It had been an exhausting day, but Rayne had promised her therapist that she would try to get a swim in. "Um, actually, I was going to go swimming if that's okay," Rayne said when she was finished with her pizza.

"Sure, that's fine, sweetheart. Like I said, I want you to feel like you can do whatever you want to while you are here." Walt was getting more and more convinced that he wanted the 'while she was here' part to become far more permanent than it was supposed to be at the beginning of this whole thing. Even on a shitty day, they came home and just relaxed together. They had held hands some, nothing extremely passionate, but it was something that made him feel connected to her. He hoped that she had gotten some strength from him just being there for her. He had felt better having her there to share dinner with last night. And even today after such a tough day, he felt better just knowing that there was someone there with him sharing a pizza and a glass of wine. "Hey, you know what? Maybe I'll join you, if you don't mind," Walt said as she was walking to her room to change. "Maybe after you get your laps done, we can unwind a little in the hot tub."

She had turned when he started talking, her face lit up like it hadn't all day so far. "That sounds great, Walt. I'll see you out there in a few minutes."

Walt jogged upstairs and put on his swim trunks. He was already in the pool when Rayne made her way out the back doors onto the deck. Damn, it was a shame he had to be so careful, because her in that bathing suit had his mind racing with all sorts of things he would like to do if he wasn't trying to be professional. He forced himself to stop staring at the beauty that was making her way into the pool and tried to act friendly, not overly fondly.

They swam laps, and Walt paced himself so that he stayed beside Rayne. He could have gone much faster, but he was sure she was doing the best she could with her legs not being very strong yet. After they swam several laps, they moved to the hot tub to relax. Walt was just so amazed at how easy they fit together. They could be talking or just sitting silently, and it all felt normal. After they had been in the hot tub for about fifteen or twenty minutes, Rayne started drifting off. Walt got out of the hot tub and she started to stir to try to get out herself. Walt put a hand on her shoulder and said, "Sweetheart, let me carry you inside. You've had one hell of a day, and you're exhausted. Just let me take care of you for tonight, please."

Rayne felt like a cooked spaghetti noodle and really didn't have the strength to argue. Besides, she really did enjoy being in his arms. Whether he was carrying her or dancing with her, his arms were a place she loved to be. "Okay," she agreed. "I won't argue with you on that. I am pretty tired."

Walt picked her up and set her on the edge of the hot tub, then he got a towel and helped her dry herself off before lifting her and carrying her into the house and to her bedroom. He put her down gently and braced her until she got her footing under her.

"Thank you for helping me at least make the end of a very long and difficult day enjoyable," she said.

"You're welcome, sweetheart. I'll see you in the morning. Hopefully we only have one more day of the really hard stuff," he encouraged. He leaned in and kissed the top of her head before walking out the door and locking up the house before heading upstairs to his own room. As long and as difficult as the day had been, he had a feeling he wasn't going to be falling asleep anytime soon. He had too much on his mind right now.

The next two days were pretty much more of the same. Expert testimony, eyewitness testimony, support from Sunni at her back and glances from Walt trying to reassure her that she would get through this. The evenings were basically the same too. The type of food varied, but the swimming and hot tub happened after relaxing for a bit. Rayne couldn't meet with her therapist on the long court days, so she made herself swim laps to try to keep up her strength.

On Wednesday night, while sitting in the hot tub, Walt began to try to prepare Rayne for the fact that she would most likely be taking the stand to tell her story on the following Tuesday. They weren't scheduled to be in court on Friday and Walt felt that he had enough information to fill Monday with other testimony. If he finished early on Monday, he would ask for a recess until the following morning so that Rayne could begin fresh and new on Tuesday morning. "I know this will be one of the hardest things you have ever had to do, sweetheart, but you will have to tell your story. The judge and the jury deserve to hear it in your words," Walt encouraged.

"I'll cry," Rayne said, the tears already there in her eyes.

"Crying is okay, sweetheart. It's your honest emotion. Just let me lead you through it. I will be right there. You know that the questions I ask will be things we have already talked about." Walt hesitated and then added, "But their attorney gets to cross examine you when I am done. And sweetheart, I will be honest, that won't be pretty. He will try to discredit your story and make it sound like you are just in this for the money." He lifted her chin, so she was looking at him face to face, the tears in her eyes almost making him want to cry. "I'll be there. Any time you need me, you just look up at me and I will do my best to send you as much strength as I possibly can. Sunni will be there too. We will do anything we can to help you get through this." He pulled her body close to his. He knew he needed to keep it professional, but a hug was okay, right? He could hold her and give her some of his strength without it being inappropriate.

When it seemed like maybe her crying was letting up, he let her go, although he kept one arm around her. "On another note, I think tomorrow during the lunch break, we should go outside and talk to the reporters." He felt her stiffen and knew she was going to protest. "Just listen, please." When she closed her mouth and nodded, he continued, "If we go in tomorrow just as we usually do, we will have lunch brought in like always, but we will go outside the courthouse to talk to the press, just before court is to return to session. That way we control the timing. Five, maybe ten minutes tops. I will do most of the talking and answer what questions I feel will be good ones to answer and avoid the ones that we don't want to get into. We will prepare a statement for you to say. Simply who you are, why you feel you deserve to win, simple things like that." He took a breath and continued, "We want you to be human to them. So far, you're just someone they heard some stories about, and I guarantee, the construction company attorney is speaking to them and he is not making you sound like a good person at all." He smiled at her and then he brushed a lock of hair from her face. "Let them see the beautiful strong woman that I see, the one that I fell for the day I walked into that rehabilitation facility. We make our statements, answer a few questions and then excuse ourselves because court is going back into session and we can't be late. Trust me on this, Rayne. I will make it work to our advantage."

She hesitated for a bit, but finally she gave a brief nod and agreed to what he was suggesting. She didn't sleep much that night; a sense of worry over all the things coming in the next several days made it impossible. Would she be able to handle the reporters? Would she totally lose it on the witness stand? When would this all be over? She knew that once Walt was done with his witnesses, the other side got to start their rebuttal and produce their own expert testimony. And undoubtedly, the employees and owners of the construction company would have their say on the whole situation. She didn't see an end to all this nightmare anytime soon.

The morning went like all mornings since this court case began. Breakfast at the breakfast bar while talking about what the day had in store. Walt gave her a written statement that she could either read or try to learn and paraphrase for the reporters they would talk to at lunchtime. She decided to try to at least have it memorized to a point. It would probably come across as stuffy if she read it, but if she could speak as if it was from the heart, she would seem more genuine.

Over the course of the morning, Rayne glanced at the statement as often as possible. Walt really had done a good job of writing something that represented her story well. She had placed it on the table and looked at it often to not only prepare herself for the interview but to drown out yet one more 'expert' who supposedly knew so much about her and her case. By the time lunch rolled around, she didn't necessarily feel confident about the interview, but she felt as prepared as she possibly could be. She picked at the salad she had asked Walt to get for her. Her stomach couldn't handle food at this point; the butterflies were too big.

As promised, Walt waited until there were only about twelve minutes before court would be back in session before he escorted her to the front of the building to face the reporters. It gave them just enough time for her to make her statement, which of course had them asking rapid-fire questions at her that Walt handled with professionalism and grace before he looked at his watch and told the reporters they were due in court and needed to go. All in all, it hadn't been as horrible as she had anticipated it would be. She did get choked up when making her statement, but that was probably to be expected. She knew that brief statement would be nothing compared to the cross examination that would come sometime next week when the opposing counsel got a chance at her on the witness stand.

Since it was Thursday and they wouldn't be in court on Friday, they had the long weekend to look forward to. They decided that they really should go home and make one of the meals that Mrs. Steele had left for them rather than eat out again. They didn't need to worry about being in bed quite as early and it might be nice to just not think about court for an evening.

At dinner, Walt praised her for how well she had handled the reporters and how well she was holding up despite how hard some of the testimony must have been on her. He knew from experience that the worst was yet to come, though. Listening to everyone else talk about her and her case and what had happened to her was never easy, but sitting up there telling the story herself was always beyond painful.

They agreed to meet in the living room to chill with a movie after they both went and got into something more comfortable. For a few days at least, the case didn't have to be at the forefront of their minds. They could take a break and just be.

Chapter Fourteen

Walt was in the living room waiting for Rayne to help him pick the movie when he saw his father's number on his caller ID. He took a deep breath before answering the phone. He and his father had an okay relationship, it wasn't close, but it wasn't horribly strained either. Generally, if it was something family related, his mom called. If his dad was calling, it usually had something to do with the law firm. After all, his father was one of the founding partners and therefore, also Walt's boss in a way. "Hello?"

His father didn't acknowledge the greeting, he simply started in on his reason for calling. "Listen, Walt, we need to talk. This is serious business you are messing with." His father barely took a breath before continuing. "I hear you are getting way too close to your client. I also hear that she is living at your house. Do you realize that opens us up for a huge lawsuit for impropriety, not to mention possible censure? We can't afford to have this go wrong."

"I know, Dad. I'm not doing anything improper here. I'm simply trying to help my client in the best way that I know how," Walt explained.

"Well, is she or is she not living at your house?" his father asked.

"She is staying at my house, in THE GUEST ROOM, yes," Walt admitted.

"Why on earth would you set us up for a lawsuit by doing that? Look, I understand. If you like the girl, that's great, but wait until after the case is over. This could go down with serious repercussions against not only you, but the firm," his dad argued.

"Dad, it's not like that. Yes, I find her attractive, but we aren't doing anything improper. I asked her to stay here because she lives in a third-floor walkup. She can't climb the stairs right now. I have a first-floor guest room that just sits here empty all the time. It was a matter of convenience for her to be able to stay close by," Walt stated.

"I'm sure she has family or friends she could stay with," his father groused.

"No family and her only real friend lives in the apartment right next door to her, you know, in the third-floor walkup apartment," Walt finished sarcastically.

"But, still, you can't be doing this, son. You have to keep yourself completely professional," his father reprimanded.

Walt was getting tired of this conversation. "Look, Dad, I'm not doing anything wrong. I'm not opening us up for a lawsuit or for formal reprimands. I'm simply helping a client. You have nothing to worry about." Walt hung up the phone. He needed some fresh air, so he left a note on the coffee table letting Rayne know that he had to go out for a bit. He headed out the front door to where his car was parked. He put the top down and cruised out of the driveway.

Rayne was in the kitchen when she heard a raised voice in the living room, so she moved closer to the door to try to hear who was so upset. From what she heard, she could tell that Walt was getting yelled at because of the things he was doing for her. She was getting him in trouble with his father. She thought she heard the front door open and then she heard the engine of Walt's little sports car start up. She moved quietly to her room and called Sunni. "Hey, Sunni," she said, trying to sound cheerful. "I was wondering if you could come and pick me up. It's not working out for me staying here at Walt's house."

"Um, okay, but why is it not working out and where will you go?" Sunni asked.

"I have a little money. I can stay in a cheap hotel for a few days. Hopefully I'll be able to go home soon. I'm getting better every day. I just can't stay here. It's just not working anymore." She wasn't sure exactly what she was going to do or where she was going to go, but she knew she couldn't stay here and cause problems for Walt.

"Okay, then, I'll be right over." Sunni sounded confused, but Rayne couldn't blame her. As far as her friend knew, staying with Walt had been something that Rayne was really enjoying. It was giving them a chance to really connect, but without the pressure of a sexual relationship.

Rayne hung up the phone. She felt the tears beginning to form at the back of her eyes. She refused to cry. She would make Sunni believe that this was a good thing, that it was what she wanted, that it was for the best. Walt had done so much for her, there was no way she could stay here and cause more problems for him with his father. She started packing a suitcase with her clothes and toiletries. She would get the rest when she could climb the stairs to her apartment again. By the time Sunni arrived, she had her bags packed and was waiting in the kitchen. She was relieved that Walt hadn't returned yet. She didn't want to have to explain why she was leaving to him; having to try to come up with a story for Sunni was going to be bad enough.

When she got into Sunni's car, she tried to act happy and nonchalant. She wasn't sure she was pulling it off, but thankfully, her friend would let it slide. She might ask a few questions, but in the end, Rayne knew that she would just accept what Rayne had felt was the right thing for her to do.

As suspected, once they pulled out of the driveway, Sunni started the questions. "Did you and Walt have a fight or something?"

"No," Rayne replied succinctly.

"Okay, then, did he try something, like come on too strong, or push you to do something you weren't comfortable with?" Sunni asked.

"No, it wasn't anything like that. I was just feeling weird living with someone I barely know. I'm sure Walt had to have been feeling the same. So I just figured it was time I do us both a favor and make other arrangements." Rayne tried to sound as convincing as she could.

Sunni looked at her and then said, "Okay." She didn't look or sound convinced, but Rayne could also tell that her friend was choosing to support her decision, even if she didn't understand it or think it was the right one.

Rayne pulled open her smart phone and began searching for a hotel that would be on the bus route so she could make it to court on Monday that also didn't cost an arm and a leg and wasn't in a neighborhood where she would be afraid to walk down the block at night. Not that she usually went out late, but she just didn't want to be in that type of neighborhood.

After Sunni helped her get settled, she asked Rayne if she wanted her to stay for a bit, or if there was anywhere else she needed to go. Rayne wasn't feeling up to having to try to put up a good front anymore, so she told her friend that she was tired and would probably lie down and take a nap. She wasn't tired, but being in her current physical condition, no one would blame her if she was. Her strength was returning, but she was by no means fully up to par yet.

She walked Sunni to the door and told her, "Listen, if Walt calls, don't tell him where I am, okay? Just let him know that I will be in court for sure on Monday." Due to the court calendar, Rayne wasn't scheduled to be there on Friday, so she had a three-day weekend to get through before she saw Walt again. Hopefully by then she would be able to seem like this was all for the best.

Sunni agreed to Rayne's request. "I just wish you would tell me what happened. But you know where I am if you need me," Sunni said. She gave her friend a hug and headed back to her car.

Rayne's phone started buzzing. She looked at the caller ID and saw that it was Walt. He was probably really confused by her not being there when he got home, but she didn't have the strength to answer the phone and try to keep up the story of this being something she was doing for herself. She let the call go to voicemail. He obviously left a message and then a few seconds later a text came through.

Hey, I got back, and you weren't here. Did you decide to go out with Sunni or something? LMK

She knew she had to give him some sort of explanation or he would be worried, and he would never let it go. So she responded to his text. She started to type *I just realized that I wasn't comfortable*, but she deleted that Walt had never done anything to make her uncomfortable. She tried again. *I just needed to have some space.* Again, not the truth, so she deleted that and started again. *I didn't feel right staying there.* Again, another lie. None of those things were true so in the end, the only text she could send that resembled the truth was:

I had Sunni pick me up, I just thought it was better if I didn't stay there right now.

After sending the text, she turned her phone off. She wouldn't be able to keep trying to say things that wouldn't give away her real reasons for leaving. Walt had been nothing but the perfect host to her. He had never made her feel uncomfortable or unwanted. In fact, he had done just the opposite; he had made her feel accepted and wanted and maybe even a little bit loved. It was best if he thought she had decided it was better for her than for her to tell him that she was doing it for him. Knowing him, he would argue that point and tell her she didn't need to leave for his sake. She knew this was for the best, though. She wouldn't be the reason he had problems with his family.

Walt read her text, which made absolutely zero sense to him, so he called Sunni. When she picked up, he asked "Hey, Sunni, is Rayne with you? She texted me that she had you pick her up. I'd like to talk to her if I can."

Sunni hesitated before responding, "Hi Walt, no, she's not with me. She had me pick her up, but I dropped her off a few minutes ago."

"Where did you drop her off and do you know when she plans to come back?" Walt asked.

"I can't tell you where I dropped her off. She asked me not to. I can tell you that she will be there for court on time Monday. She said to be sure to tell you that," Sunni said.

"I don't care about court on Monday, I need to know where she is. Come on, Sunni, you know I only want the best for her," Walt pleaded.

"I know, and believe me, I don't agree with her choice to leave. She didn't tell me why she needed to go, only that she did." Sunni hesitated and then added, "I know you are good for her, Walt. Don't give up on her, but for whatever reason, this is just something that she needed to do, and we have to respect that."

Walt didn't want to 'respect' anything that took Rayne out of his life. That was why he had basically told his dad to back off. However, he also knew that if he pushed for his desires instead of respecting her choices, he wasn't much of a man and he certainly couldn't hope to win her back over some day if he pushed her now. "Okay, yeah, I get it. But, if she needs anything, you let me know, okay?"

"I will Walt. I think there is just a lot going on in her head right now and she needs to process."

"You don't think me pushing her to talk to the reporters is what scared her off, do you?" Walt was suddenly worried. He had thought the interview had gone perfectly. Rayne had come across as a strong woman who had been dealt a nasty blow and deserved some sort of justice. She hadn't seemed like she was looking for some huge payout just so she could get rich.

"No, I don't think that's it," Sunni assured him. "Look, Walt, you really are the first man that she has spent any real time with. She doesn't know how to do relationships. Just give her some time. I'll be there for her if she decides she wants to talk and if she has any problems come up, I'll let you know. I just have to respect the fact that she asked me to keep her location a secret for now."

Walt didn't like it, but what else could he do? He told Sunni he understood and hung up the phone. He walked into Rayne's room to see just how much of her things she had taken with her. Did she just pack a few things and would have to be back in a few days, or had she moved completely out of his house? He was happy to find that all that seemed to be missing were her clothes and the things she had kept in the bathroom.

Walt noticed a box that was labeled 'pictures' and started looking through it. Sure, it was an invasion of her privacy, but he really did want some sort of connection to her and pictures were all he had. As he went through them, he realized that he wanted her to be in his life and in his home hopefully for a long time to come. He took a picture of her with her parents and one of her and Sunni. The one had been taken probably a decade before, she was so young sitting there smiling with her parents on what appeared to be Christmas morning. The other was much more recent. It appeared to be a picture of a time when Rayne and Sunni had made their way to one of the beaches along the Lake Michigan shoreline. He took them out to his living room and placed the one of her parents on the mantle and the one with Sunni on the shelving unit beside the TV. He stood back and looked at them. Yes, he decided, Rayne belonged in his home. He went back and got more pictures from the box and started finding places for the ones he thought she would find most special. He found a picture of just Rayne. She was beautiful. It looked like maybe she had just finished a dance recital or something. It wasn't very old; she looked exactly as she did now. He took that one and raced upstairs to put it on the nightstand beside his bed. She would be the last thing he saw every night and the first thing he saw every morning. The pictures would just have to do until he could convince her to move back in with him.

After he had placed a few more pictures around his home, he decided that he would pour himself a glass of scotch. He really was more of a beer man—that's why he was part owner of a brewery—and with Rayne, they often had a glass of wine. But, something about tonight told him that it was a night for scotch if he had any hope of sleeping at all. He had a pretty decent liquor cabinet for those times when his parents came over or when he had needed to host a small dinner for clients or partners from the firm. He poured one glass and downed it right away. He poured a second and went out to the back deck to watch the sky turn to the darkest of night while sipping his scotch. He couldn't help but wonder what could have possibly gone wrong. When he finally went to bed, he had apparently had enough scotch that he was able to get a few hours of sleep before his restlessness got him back up.

Rayne had gotten Sunni to stop at a store for a few things before she had dropped her off at the hotel. Rayne knew she couldn't afford to eat out on top of the hotel bill, so she had bought things that she could munch on over the next few days. She had also indulged herself and gotten a box of wine. Well, indulged wasn't really the word for it since it was cheap wine, but it was wine nonetheless. It was nothing like some of the wonderful wines she had tried since coming to know Walt. Thursday night before going to bed, she had indulged in a couple of glasses and that was probably a big part of why she had been able to sleep at least a little bit of the night.

When Rayne woke up Friday morning, she knew that she couldn't just sit and sulk and miss Walt. She needed to keep her therapy up or she was going to suffer. She went down to use the pool so she could swim laps. She pushed herself to swim as strong as she could for as long as she could. She was hoping that pushing herself physically would help her not think about Walt. She was wrong. All she thought about were the times that they had swum laps together in his pool. The times he had said "race ya" and she knew he didn't even try to win. With her reduced strength, there was no way that a man who was as physically fit as Walt wouldn't beat her in a true race. Still, she pushed herself to exhaustion hoping to find some relief from the thoughts tormenting her mind.

Walt woke up early on Friday and decided that he should go to the office. Even though Rayne's case was the only one that he was really focusing on now, he had other small things he could be working on. Maybe it would keep his mind focused on something else for the day at least. He decided that if he couldn't find Rayne, he might be spending most of his time either at the office or the brewery for the weekend. Maybe some serious gym time too.

Walt heard a knock on the open door of his office and looked up to see Zak standing there. He motioned for him to come in. "Hey, what's up?" Walt asked.

"That was what I was wondering," Zak replied. "I haven't seen you in the office much at all lately. I know you've been in court this week, but you kind of fell off the face of the earth for a couple of weeks now. I figured you were having fun with your girl from the whole wind chime escapade."

"I was, but she's also a client, so she can't really be my girlfriend at this point," Walt explained.

"Ah, gotcha. Well if you need me to step in and pick up some of the workload just let me know. And, if you want someone to keep the girl busy, I am sure I could handle that too," Zak joked.

"Yeah, you stay away from Rayne, I know how you keep women

busy," Walt rebuffed.

Zak held up his hands and surrendered. "Just offering." He walked back out the door.

Zak had given him something to think about. Zak was a personal injury lawyer too. If things got too sticky, he could have Zak take over the case or step in as co-counsel. No way was he allowing Zak to hang out with Rayne in anything but a professional capacity. All the sloth guys tended to be playboys to a point. Zak was truly the biggest one, though. Walt didn't think Zak had ever been with any woman more than one time. He really stood by his 'one and done' policy.

Jeremy was probably the most chaste of them all. He was the son of a well-known senator and worked in his dad's office. He still spent time with women, but either he was good at keeping it hidden or he only dated the 'right kind of women,' as their fathers would call them.

Pete was a criminal law attorney here at the firm and the son of a founding partner. He wasn't quite as careful as Jeremy, but they all knew how much they could and couldn't do without bringing down the wrath of the senior partners.

Jason was the luckiest of them all in the dating aspect of life. He was a business management wiz, so he was the one who took care of the day-to-day operations of Five Sloths. They all spent time there to meet patrons and such, but Jason was the one that kept the business running smoothly.

Walt ended up spending all his time out of the house other than coming home at night, taking a shower, grabbing some scotch and going to bed.

Rayne had talked to Sunni every few hours during the day. Her friend was a true friend indeed. She didn't ask what had happened at Walt's house; she just offered her support and a shoulder if it was needed. Sunday night, Sunni convinced Rayne to at least let her bring over a pizza so they could hang out. She had brought clothes with her too and when she got there, she suggested they have a slumber party for two and then they could just go to court together in the morning. Rayne agreed. It would be nice having the company.

After the pizza and the bottle of wine Sunni had bought, Rayne finally broke down and told Sunni what she had overheard. Sunni said she understood, but maybe Rayne should give Walt a chance to explain, or at least let him know why she had left. Sunni was worried that Walt would be blaming himself and thinking that he had hurt or offended Rayne in some way. She told Rayne that he had asked if having her talk to the reporters had been a bad idea. Rayne agreed that she would do her best to try to reassure Walt that it wasn't anything he had done wrong, but she refused to tell him what had made her leave in the first place. She didn't want to cause more issues between Walt and his father.

Chapter Fifteen

Monday morning started out for Walt the same way court mornings always had—well, court mornings before Rayne had moved in. It was odd how in such a short time his 'new normal' had become what he wanted to have far more than his 'old normal'. He had his usual coffee and omelet. He had had to dump half of it in the trash because he had cracked twice as many eggs as he needed because he had been planning on making one for Rayne too.

He got to the courthouse extra early so that he would wait outside to make sure Rayne didn't have any problems with reporters or with security. When she and Sunni walked up, he had the urge to pull her to him and hold her, but he knew he couldn't do that. Instead, he settled for placing a hand at the small of her back and starting to lead her down the hall toward the elevator. He leaned over and said, "It's so good to see you, sweetheart, but we really need to talk about this. I'm willing to meet you on neutral ground, wherever you want, but we need to talk." He didn't push it any further, but he wasn't going to let this drop either.

The afternoon ended early when Walt finished up with his last expert witness. He asked the judge if they could adjourn until morning so that his client could be rested and fresh before she had to take the stand to testify on her own behalf. The judge looked her way and she must have seemed sufficiently exhausted because he said they would begin again at 10:00 a.m. the next morning. Rayne stood and started to head out the door before Walt could get a chance to stop her, but she didn't succeed. He caught her gently by the arm and pulled her to the side so no one else could hear their conversation.

"I don't know what's going on here Rayne. I feel like I have done something wrong, but I have no clue what it was. Talk to me, tell me what happened," Walt pleaded.

"Nothing is wrong," Rayne stated. She was pretty sure her voice didn't sound any more convincing to him than it did to her, but she had to be firm on this. She couldn't cause him problems with his father or with his job. "I just couldn't stay at your place anymore, it wasn't right. If you'll excuse me, Sunni is waiting to give me a ride home." She skirted away before he had a chance to say anything else. It wouldn't look good to desperately grab his client, so he let her go.

Walt tried to follow them down the hall. He at least wanted to help her get through the throng of reporters outside. But as he stepped into the hallway, he heard someone call out his name. He turned to see a woman, probably in her mid-60s, standing there looking at him like she desperately needed to talk to him.

"Yes, can I help you?" he asked.

"Well, I am hoping that maybe I can help you," she stated. "Or more accurately, I am hoping that I can help your client. She's such a beautiful young thing and she doesn't deserve what happened to her."

Walt was starting to wonder if this person was a reporter that had somehow gotten past security or if it was some quack that thought she could somehow rid the world of all the wrongs in it. "Ah, yes, well, I really need to be going," Walt said, reaching in his pocket for a business card. "Why don't you call my office and schedule an appointment and we can talk then." Walt knew his administrative assistant was good at weeding out the crazies and he would never really have to have an appointment with this woman.

However, she obviously wasn't one to be brushed off so easily. "I think I have some information that you need to know. I saw the two young men that work for the construction company having lunch that day. Right before your client was injured. "

"Ah, well, okay, um." Walt wasn't sure what to say. Seeing the man at lunch wasn't helpful, but somehow this woman wouldn't let it go.

"I also saw the four beers that they each had with lunch," she added.

That got Walt's attention. If the men had been drinking, this might just be a whole new ballgame. "Four beers, you say?"

"Yes, and not those little sample ones like you get at breweries nowadays. These were full glasses of beer. I also heard one of them tell his buddy that they needed to get going because if they didn't have that truck loaded up by the time the supervisor was ready, the boss was going to give them hell." She was shaking her head as she continued. "He was slurring his words; he had obviously had too much to drink. One of his other buddies gave him some mints or something and told him that he better make sure his breath didn't smell like beer. They also told him he probably shouldn't say much to the boss until he could talk without sounding like he had been drinking." She took a breath before continuing. "Then the two of them got up and headed out the door. They weren't exactly walking straight lines either."

"Uh, wow," Walt said. "That's quite the story. I'm not sure we have a way of proving that though."

"Oh, I have that too," she said, rifling through her purse. "I didn't really think much of it at the time. Other than to think that they were irresponsible young men." She pulled out a slip of paper that looked like a receipt. "When I got my slip back from the waitress, there were two stuck together." She held up the paper. "See, right here, two bacon cheeseburgers, one order of fries, one order of onion rings and eight beers."

Walt wasn't sure why the woman had kept a receipt that wasn't hers, but it just might be a godsend that she had. Walt took the receipt and looked at the date. It matched. The time was just under an hour before the accident had occurred. Which, given the time it would take the two to load up the piping, put it in the exact right timeline to make someone—no, two someones—look awfully suspicious of negligence because of intoxication. And, since he had put it on a credit card, the name was on the receipt as well. It might not have the other man's name, but it had at least one of the employees who were loading that truck.

"And you would be willing to testify to this in court?" Walt asked.

"Oh, why, yes, of course!" she exclaimed. "When I saw that young woman on the news the other day, my heart broke for her. I don't know why but over the weekend, the more I thought about things, the more it seemed to stick in my mind that there was something about this that was familiar. I realized it was the name of the construction company. Those men had it on their shirts. That was when I put it all together and started looking for the receipt to see if the dates matched."

He held up the receipt and asked, "Would you be okay with me keeping this so that it can be submitted as evidence if need be?"

"Oh, yes, definitely," she agreed.

"Great, thank you so much." Walt reached into the side pocket of his briefcase and pulled out a pad of paper and a pen from his pocket. "Would you give me your name and contact information, in case we do need to call you into testify?" Just as he started to hand her the paper, he saw his opposing counsel walking down the hall and an idea hit him. "On second thought, would you be willing to tell your story again to a fellow attorney?"

Her face lit with a smile, "Why yes, of course I will, and I'll give you my information too."

Walt called out for the other attorney, who stopped and turned around to see what it was that Walt wanted. Walt took the woman's arm and escorted her toward the other man. "What was your name, ma'am?" he asked just before they reached each other.

"Esther Nielsen," she said.

"Great." Walt gave her a big smile and then turned to the man standing impatiently waiting to see what they wanted him for. "Hi, Stevens. I'd like you to meet someone. This is Esther, she has a really fascinating story that I would really like her to share with you." He turned to Esther and nodded for her to go ahead and tell her story.

Stevens kind of paled a little as the story went on and he got pale when Walt held up the receipt showing the eight beers. Walt also pointed out the date and time frame of what had obviously happened. The employees had been drunk, they hadn't fastened the piping on correctly, and Rayne had suffered for it.

Stevens sort of spit and sputtered at first before finally saying, "I'll talk to my client and get back to you." Then he started to scurry off.

Walt knew that the attorney couldn't make any decision on whether or not to settle the case, but he also knew the man was smart enough to see that this would not go well for them if they finished it out in a court battle. "Great, I look forward to hearing from you," Walt shouted down the hall, then added, "Tonight. My client is set to start her testimony tomorrow morning and the more she has to sit through will be more we will expect when this settles."

The man was obviously smart. He quickly said, "Got it" and headed out the door. Walt had no doubt he would hear from the man in the next few hours. He still took Esther's information, just in case, but if the attorney's reaction had been any indication, it wouldn't be needed. They both knew the company wasn't looking good now.

Two hours later, Walt's phone rang with his assistant's number on it. "Hello," he answered.

"Hello, Mr. Jensen, I have a phone call to put through to you if you're ready, a Mr. Stevens," she said.

Walt sat back in his deck chair with a smile. "Yes, put him through." When the call clicked through, Walt said, "Stevens, you have good news for me, I hope."

"Yes, of course. After the information you shared with me today, I obviously advised my client to settle," Stevens said. He named a figure, a pretty decent figure in Walt's estimation. It was less than what they had gone after in court, but settlements usually were, and there were never any guarantees what the jury would decide. A settlement of any amount that came even close to the original demand was a good offer. This one was not anything to sneeze at.

"I'll have to run this past my client, of course," Walt stated. "I'll let you know before 9 in the morning, so you know whether or not we have to be in court." Walt knew he was being a bit of an ass; after all, he could get Rayne's answer way before tomorrow morning—well, he could find her, that was. But he wanted to take the opportunity to make the opposition squirm just a little longer. He was pretty sure Rayne would take the offer. She really didn't want to have to get up on that stand, and the offer was a pretty decent one.

Stevens didn't sound quite so sure of himself as he usually did when he said, "Oh, yes, of course, just let me know." Then he hung up.

Now to find himself one little ballerina. They had lots to talk about. If she took this deal, he wouldn't be her attorney anymore after the paperwork got signed tomorrow. He called Sunni because he was pretty sure Rayne wouldn't answer. When she picked up the phone, he tried to sound very businesslike. "Look, Sunni, I need you to get me in touch with Rayne. It's about the case. There has been a development and I need to speak to her. It's urgent. Do you know where she is or how to contact her?"

Sunni was slightly confused by his businesslike tone, so it took her a few seconds to respond. "Uh, yeah, I know where she is. I can get a hold of her. Do you need her to call you?"

"No, this needs to be done in person. It can be public if she wants it to be, but I really need to talk to her like within the next hour." He was lying just a little. He had until tomorrow morning before he HAD to have her answer; he just wanted to see her sooner so this whole thing could be over.

"Okay, I'll call her and one of us will call you back to set up the meet," Sunni said, then she added, "You aren't doing this to set her up just to see you, are you, Walt? Because that would be a really shitty thing to do."

"Look, Sunni, I won't deny that I really want to see Rayne and I want to hold her and talk to her and try to figure out what is going on, but this really is about the case. There has been a development and I need to know which way she wants us to go on this," Walt assured her.

"Okay, give me a few," Sunni said before hanging up.

Walt made sure he was all ready to go as soon as Sunni called him back. When she called and told him that Rayne had agreed to meet him at Five Sloths, his own brewery, he was sure he had her. They both had memories of a first date there, of their first dance. He could use this to his advantage and hopefully not only end this case but start focusing on their life. He got in his car and called ahead to let the hostess know that he needed the private table that they kept available for themselves. By the time he got to the pub, he was feeling mighty fine. He waited outside for Sunni and Rayne to arrive. When they got there, he escorted them inside and to their table.

"Why don't we order before we get down to business?" Walt said.

They each took a menu, although Walt didn't need one. He did it more to try to calm himself down than anything. He really wanted this to look like he wasn't desperately hoping for this case to be over. He had to be professional and let the client decide what she wanted to do with this offer. What he wanted was completely irrelevant at this point in the game.

After they had placed their order, Rayne turned to Walt and asked nervously, "So, what is this about my case? Has there been a problem?"

"No, no problem," Walt assured her. "Actually, we had a witness come forward late in the day that had some information that could be a total game changer. I approached the opposing counsel, and his client has come back with an offer to settle." Rayne looked up at him expectantly, but he had to play this by the book. "This offer isn't near what we had asked for in the lawsuit. But if we continue with the case, there is no guarantee that we will win, or if we win what amount the jury will deem fit to award. It's a lot to consider, Rayne, and only you can make the decision. Of course, I am sure Sunni will be glad to offer advice, but as your attorney, I have to remain completely out of the decision-making process."

"And if I take this settlement, what then? What happens to the court case?" she asked. She really was nervous about having to be on the stand.

"If you take it, we set up a meeting tomorrow either in a conference room at the courthouse or at a conference room in my office and we sign some paperwork stipulating what amount is agreed to, how long they have to pay it, things like that," he said.

"And I don't have to go back to court at all, no more experts, no more questions, it's done?" She sounded like she would probably take the offer even if it was five bucks if it got her out of that courtroom.

"Exactly. The case ends the minute the paperwork is signed other than waiting on payment and me having to file some things. But as far as you're concerned, it ends when the paperwork is signed," Walt assured her.

Rayne was looking at the table sort of shaking her head like she couldn't believe that was possible. That it really could be over for her in a matter of hours, not days and days. "Over, all over," she mumbled, and then she mumbled something that sounded sort of like, "And your father..." but she trailed off as if she had realized that she'd said something she shouldn't have.

"My father?" Walt asked, "Did you say something about my father? Did my father do something to you, Rayne? What did he say? When did he get to you? Is this why..." He trailed off. If his father had gotten to her, it would explain so many things.

"No, I've never met your father," Rayne assured him.

"Then why did you start to say something about him?" Walt was puzzled. This was not making any sense.

Rayne seemed hesitant to say anything, but finally, Sunni nudged her and said, "You have to tell him, Rayne. He has a right to know what happened."

Rayne looked up into Walt's gorgeous green eyes and realized that she really did need to do this. He had a right to know why she had walked out. She had been miserable, and from the dark circles under his eyes, he hadn't been fairing much better. It was time to tell the truth. "I overheard you on the phone with him on Thursday night," she stated simply.

"And you thought you needed to leave." Walt was nodding; he got it now. She had no idea that his dad basically overreacted to anything that was even a possible perceived threat to the law firm or his ability to make more money. She had a father that doted on her and one that she was close to. She had no way of understanding that his father just wasn't like that. "Let's get a couple of things straight here, sweetheart. My dad is sometimes an overzealous blowhard. If he thinks that the firm has even the most minute chance of losing money, he will try everything in his power to stop that from happening. Secondly, I didn't do anything that would have gotten me in trouble, I was very careful with that. Although I will admit, I am hoping we can see where things go after this is over, whether you take the settlement or not." He reached over and took her chin firmly in his hand and leaned in so that they were almost nose to nose. "And the bottom line of all this is that the only person who could accuse me of wrongdoing is you. And I'm really hoping you don't have a problem with me wanting to get to know you better."

Rayne flushed; she didn't know what to say. The case wasn't truly over yet, although it might be by tomorrow. She knew he didn't think he would get in trouble, but she still wouldn't be the one who caused an issue between Walt and his father. She just had to turn away; this was getting too intense. She looked at Sunni, hoping her friend would offer some sort of distraction from the heavy conversation.

Sunni came to her rescue as usual. "So, about this settlement offer. I'm dying to know what they are willing to put up to keep this from going any further."

That seemed to pull him out of his staring at Rayne and returned him back to his professional status. "Right, sorry. They offered 15."

Rayne's eyes went wide, and she was blinking. "They offered fifteen thousand dollars for this to all go away?" She sounded amazed. Sunni looked a little impressed with that figure too.

Walt started to chuckle a little. Oh, this was going to be fun. "No, sorry, Rayne, they didn't offer $15,000. What they offered was fifteen MILLION dollars."

Rayne's eyes got as big as saucers, and Sunni spat out the drink of water she had just started to take.

"Fifteen....mil...." Rayne shook her head. "Fifteen....million... dollars. I don't even know what fifteen million dollars looks like."

"Of course, you have to pay your attorney. But I think I can get the firm to give you the friends and family discount," Walt said with a wink. He was going to talk to his dad and after what he had almost cost him, this was going to be one hell of a discount. Their food arrived, but Rayne still looked like she was so overwhelmed that she couldn't eat. Walt and Sunni had no such problems. Walt was finally able to eat again after the way he had been picking at his food since Rayne had left him. Walt and Sunni made small talk while they ate so that Rayne could try to digest what he had just told her.

When they had finished eating, Walt said, "Not to be a nag here, but have you made a decision about the offer yet, Rayne? If not, that's fine, but we really should let them know before court tomorrow at 10:00 if they need to be there ready to proceed."

She looked at him, confused. "I thought that was a given. Yes, I'll take it, then this nightmare can finally start to end. Yes, yes, a thousand times, yes."

"Wonderful. I will let them know, and if you will answer your phone in the morning, I will let you know what time I set the meeting for." He was kind of teasing but also kind of not teasing. He still wasn't sure where he stood.

"Oh, trust me, I'll answer that call," she said with a smile. "Now, I have a question for you, counselor."

Walt raised his eyebrow. "And what would that be?" He wasn't sure where she was going to go with this.

Rayne smiled and stood up and put out her hand toward him. "Would you dance with me? I think I have something to celebrate."

He took her hand and rose from his seat. "I think I have a few things to celebrate myself tonight. I won a major case and hopefully, I'm on my way to getting my girlfriend back." He raised his eyebrows suggestively.

"I think you have a pretty good chance of that," she said as they faced each other on the dance floor. She didn't need as much support from him as she had that first night, but that didn't mean that she didn't want to hold him tight and be as close as possible.

Chapter Sixteen

Walt made the phone call at 8:00 in the morning. As much as he liked the idea of making his opponents squirm until the last minute, he just wanted this over so that he and Rayne could get back to seeing where things might go between them. He set the meeting for 10:00 and called to let the judge's office know that they were reaching a settlement agreement in the case. He apologized for the last-minute notice, but he told the secretary that had answered that his opponents had come in with a last-minute offer trying to settle this before proceeding any further. Heck, the judge would probably be elated; his calendar had just cleared for the day. He could be on the golf course by nine. Then he called Rayne to let her know what time the meeting was and asked if she wanted him to pick her up. He wasn't sure she would say yes because that would give away her location. But he hoped she would because he had felt like maybe they had started to reconnect last night while dancing. She told him that he could pick her up and she named the hotel she was staying at. It wasn't a great hotel, but it at least wasn't a seedy hotel either. Hopefully, she would be moving back into his house soon. He told her he would pick her up at 9:30. He almost added that she should bring her things with her, but he didn't. He wasn't going to push—well, maybe gentle nudges in the direction he wanted her to go, but he wouldn't outright push her into anything. If she gave him the chance, though, he had so many things he wanted to do with and to her.

Walt was standing beside his car in front of Rayne's hotel when she came out the door. He held out both hands and it surprised him a little when she took them and stepped into him. He gave her a quick kiss on the cheek, and she flushed a little while looking around. "It's okay, sweetheart. No one is watching and, in another hour or so, no one will care that I kissed you," Walt assured her.

She seemed to accept his reassurance and didn't pull away. She allowed him to open her door and help her into the car.

When they got to his office building, he gently guided her with a hand on her lower back toward the conference room that he had reserved for this meeting.

Rayne didn't understand much of what was discussed during the meeting; she just trusted Walt and signed where he told her to sign. She had to agree to the amount, which she was still overwhelmed with. And she had to agree to not bring any further lawsuits regarding this incident. She had to sign something called an NDA stating that she wouldn't do any interviews or write any books or talk about the incident in general. Walt had explained that she was welcome to talk about her accident, and the things that had happened to her, but she couldn't name the construction company or talk about the actual settlement with anyone. She was fine with all of that. She just wanted to put all of this behind her.

When the others had left the meeting, Walt escorted her back to his office. She had never seen it before. It was a pretty typical law office, she supposed, although she hadn't seen one of those before either. There were shelves of books, a big desk with two comfortable looking high back chairs in front of it and an area off to the corner with two long leather couches and two chairs that matched the couches. There was a coffee table in the middle. It was the perfect place to hold small intimate meetings or sit comfortably and talk about a case. Walt closed the door behind them and took both of her hands. He stood in front of her and pulled her closer so that they were eye to eye. "Now for the important conversation," Walt said. "My paralegal is on her way to the courthouse to file that paperwork and get the judge to sign off on it." He realized that it was sort of backwards that he hadn't let his paralegal really handle much of anything with this case, but as soon as the agreement was signed, he sent her on her merry way to get it filed so that he didn't have to take any more time dealing with the paperwork. "Once the judge signs off, this case is done. I am hoping that you want the same thing I want now that this is over. I hope you want to at least give the possibility of a relationship with me a try."

She nodded. "Yes, I would like to see where this could go. I have no experience with this at all, so I may get things completely wrong, but I would like to see what being your girlfriend is like," she said, smiling.

He pulled her into him for a kiss. He started out with gentle feather-like kisses on and around her mouth. He trailed a few along her jawline before coming back and kissing her lips in longer, more pressing kisses.

Soon he found himself pressing his tongue against her lips, trying to get her to open to him and she did, so sweetly, she did. He could sort of sense her lack of experience, but there definitely wasn't any hesitation or lack of enthusiasm on her part. She was kissing him back fully. When his tongue entered her mouth, she hesitated at first, like she wasn't sure what she should do, but soon, her tongue was brushing playfully against his. Her genuine passion even with her lack of experience was a heady thing. She was intoxicating and she didn't even realize just how much of a turn-on her response was to him.

The kissing got more and more involved and Walt found himself wanting so much more from her. He started to gently walk her backwards toward the long couch against the wall. When the back of her knees hit the couch, he stopped kissing her long enough to sit and then lie back on the couch. He held his hand out to her to invite her to lie with him. She was in his arms and the kissing resumed immediately. Walt found himself wanting more and more of her. His cock wanted to be freed so that it could fully explore her too, but Walt wasn't going to take this woman's virginity on the leather couch in his office. She deserved way more romance than that. In fact, he wasn't sure that she was even willing to go that far yet. They had spent hours and hours together over the last few months, but they hadn't been romantic or sexual at all before this very moment. He had to slow himself down.

He pulled away so that he could look into her eyes again. "So this is how I would like to see things go for the rest of the day. If you don't agree, please don't feel like you have to say yes, because"—he pointed to his chest—"overbearing selfish ass here, remember." When she giggled and nodded at his comment, he continued. "I would like to take you back to your hotel so that you can grab your belongings and check out. I want you back at my house, even if it is in the guest room. I will never pressure you to go any further than you are willing to go, but I have missed you so much these last few days. Even sitting with you at breakfast and dinner has become something I look forward to. I love swimming with you in the afternoons and dancing with you in the evenings. I'd like for us to go out to a nice dinner and maybe dancing somewhere to celebrate the case finally being over. How does that sound to you, sweetheart?"

Rayne acted like that was a lot to ponder and didn't answer right away. Finally, after making him sweat a bit, she said, "I want to move back in with you too. I don't know yet if I'm ready for more than the guest room or not, that I honestly must play by ear. But I don't want to go out to dinner and dancing."

He looked sort of hurt by that, so Rayne continued, "I want to have dinner and dancing at your house. I missed those things too. I swam in the hotel pool because I knew I needed the therapy, but I didn't have fun with it the way I do with you. I missed you so much," she said as she pulled herself closer to him and pressed her lips to his. They started making out again and this time, Rayne seemed even more eager.

Finally, Walt pulled away and made himself stop. If this kept going, he was going to try to seduce her right here on this couch and he vowed that he was not going to let their first time be in his office in a cold and professional environment. Rayne started to try to press in again, but he held her back. "Not now, sweetheart, and definitely not here." He smiled. "There are so many things that I want to do to you and with you, but this is not the place for them to start. Let's go get your things. I have the rest of the day free. I have the rest of the week free. I was supposed to be in court all week. Other than having to take my shift at the brewery tomorrow night, I don't have a lot on my calendar this week."

He stood up and held out a hand to help her up. She was getting so much stronger, but she still had some weakness in her legs. He never wanted her to feel like an invalid, but he also didn't want to see her struggle or in pain. As they walked out of his office, his dad just happened to be in the hallway. He hadn't noticed them; he had his face buried in the file he was reading. Walt held up a finger to Rayne and raised his eyebrows in a 'wait till you see this' gesture. "Hey, Dad!" Walt exclaimed.

His father stopped and looked up, surprised. "Oh, Walt, I didn't know you were here. I thought you had court today."

"Ah, yeah, about that." She could tell Walt was having fun with this. Walt's phone chimed with a text. It was from his paralegal; the judge had signed off. Perfect timing. "I'm not going back to court on the case."

His father looked confused. Walt had to admit, this settlement offer had gone down a lot more quickly than usual. He generally would have run it past the partners just to be sure they were okay with it. Although no one in their right mind would have said no to this one. "No, I just wanted you to meet my girlfriend. Dad, this is Rayne, Rayne, this is my father William Jensen."

Rayne put out her hand and at first, she wasn't sure the man would take it, but finally, manners got the better of his befuddlement and he shook her hand. He muttered something that sounded like "Nice to meet you," but she wasn't sure.

He looked at Walt and back at Rayne before saying, "Would you mind waiting out here for a moment? I need to talk to my son in private." Rayne dutifully went to the chair in the outer office area and waited. She hoped that Walt didn't get into too much trouble with his dad.

The worry probably showed on her face because Walt turned to her before following his father into the office and said. "Don't worry about this, and don't you dare leave." He gave her a look that challenged her to challenge him. She thought better of that and settled into her chair.

Walt followed his dad into his office. This wasn't going to go the way the old man thought.

His father turned on him. "Now, what do you mean you aren't going back to court? Did you settle or did something go wrong?" Leave it to his dad to think he had messed something up. Maybe it was time to rethink being loyal to this law firm after all.

"Yes, Dad, we settled." Walt did some calculations in his head. Originally, they had agreed to take the case for a 20% contingency fee. In most cases they asked for one third, but everyone agreed that this was a case that they were more than willing to take a cut on. Of that, the firm would get half, and he would get half. It was then his job to pay the billable hours put in by his paralegal. His administrative assistant got paid a regular wage by the firm because she worked for more than one attorney. The way he calculated it, that meant the firm would be getting a cool 1.5 million dollars out of this. He wouldn't tell his dad that he wasn't taking his half. His paralegal really hadn't done much, but he would pay her anyway. He wasn't taking money from Rayne. "Yeah, I settled. You'll be happy with 1.5 million, I'm sure."

His father looked a little skeptical. "1.5? Walt, I am sure you could have gotten more than 1.5."

"No, Dad, you don't get it. The firm gets 1.5." That seemed to have his father singing a different tune. He seemed happier now. "But one more thing, Dad. The case is over, Rayne is my girlfriend, there is no conflict of interest or chance at professionalism, so back off. If you treat Rayne as anything less than a woman that I care very deeply for, you and I will have a problem."

"Walt, I never intended to interfere with your personal life as long as your professional one was above board," his dad tried to explain.

"Well, that's great then. She is my girlfriend and I intend to keep her around. You will be seeing her at family functions and company events in the future," Walt stated.

His dad didn't seem to know how to react to that. Walt didn't think that it was because he was still upset about the professionalism. His did just didn't know how to do personal relationships all that well either. They headed back out of his office together. When they got closer, Rayne stood up. His father looked at her and said, "It was nice to meet you, Rayne. I'm sure my wife will be inviting you to dinner soon." He gave her what seemed like a genuine smile. Maybe his father could learn something.

Walt and Rayne stopped at the hotel to pick up her things after they had grabbed lunch at a local bistro. When they got to her room, the bed almost tempted Walt to try to start something again, but he held himself back. He politely leaned against the dresser while she got her toiletries and things around. When she was in the bathroom, he texted Mrs. Steele and asked if she had any recommendations for what to make for a special dinner. He knew she probably had the normal meals in the freezer like she always did, but he wasn't sure which one would be good for a special dinner. She texted back her recommendation and asked if his "friend" was coming back. He sent a smiley emoji and said yes.

As they made their way back out to Walt's car, he realized it was only about 2:00 in the afternoon. If they went home now, it would be way too early for dinner and he wasn't sure he could keep himself from starting something with her again. Despite how much he wanted to do this evening right with dinner and dancing, his body was all about getting to the more enjoyable portion of the evening. He needed to find something to do to waste a couple of hours before they went home and heated up their dinner. He figured that he could get away with claiming that he needed to do something at the brewery, check inventory or something. That should keep him out of trouble.

When Rayne was all ready to go, he escorted her to his car and as he started it, he asked, "Hey, sweetheart, since it's still early would you mind if we stopped by the brewery for a bit? Tomorrow is my night to co-manage and I just want to be sure that things are stocked so that I don't run into an issue." That sounded plausible, right?

"Oh, yeah, sure, don't let me interfere with things you need to do," she assured him. "I have some phone calls and things to make anyway."

Walt wasn't sure what phone calls she had to make; he was hoping they had nothing to do with finding a new place to live. She wouldn't have her money for a week or so, but that didn't mean she wasn't going to start looking for a place that wasn't a third-floor walkup. He was really hoping she would consider a 5-bedroom 5.5-bathroom house on the east side as possible long-term housing.

When they got to the brewery, Walt parked her on one of the stools at the bar with one of their fruity non-alcoholic drinks while he went into the office to check on a few things. Jason was already in there, of course. How could he not be? Jason was here most of the time really. He was the one that ran the brewery on a day-to-day basis. He had been the one that got his MBA. Whereas three of the five guys were attorneys, the other two had learned more toward the business side of things. Jason was the one that stepped up when they decided to invest in a microbrewery and offered to be the manager. The other "business mind" was slated to run for the Senate when his father retired someday.

Jason was the right man for the job, though. He had done wonders from the business aspect; the brewery had started turning a profit way sooner than any of them had expected. He was also an incredible flirt, which wasn't a bad thing when it came to running a business. Whether he was flirting with a woman sexually or just being a friendly host with both men and women, his charm brought in customers. The brewery was closed on Mondays. Each of the partners other than Jason had a specific night that they were there to co-manage and on Friday and Saturday, they took turns alternating. Jason ran the business during the day when they mostly only had a few people per hour after the lunch rush was over. By the time the dinner crowd started coming in, he had someone else there to help keep things running smoothly. Jason really was the person most people knew as the manager; he was great at doing the "schmooze," as he always called it. Sometimes Walt had worried that he did a little too much schmoozing with females, but they never seemed to complain.

"Hey, Jason," Walt said. "I figured I'd stop by and check in on how things are looking. I know I'm not here till tomorrow night, but I had some time to kill and I thought I'd stop by."

The office had one-way glass that looked out over the bulk of the restaurant and bar area. It was obvious when Jason perked up that he had spotted Rayne sitting at the counter. "If I had a couple of hours to kill, I certainly wouldn't be doing it here if I had a hottie like that that I could be doing," Jason joked.

Walt looked at him with a threatening glare. "Look, you don't understand, okay? Up until a few hours ago, I was her attorney and had to keep things totally professional. It's not like I'm going to jump on her five minutes after the ink is dry on her settlement."

"I don't know why. That is one hot honey. I'd be jumping her in all sorts of ways," Jason said.

Walt got up and got in Jason's face. "Look, asshole, she's a virgin, okay? I'm not going to be a barbarian and rip her clothes off at the first possible chance."

Jason backed up and put his hands up in surrender. "Chill dude, I was just messing with you." He shook his head. "How do you get so lucky, man? A gorgeous girl like that and she's a virgin, and from what I hear, about to be very rich."

"How did you...ah, wait, let me guess, Sunni?" Walt asked.

"Yeah, she might have mentioned it when I called her earlier today," Jason admitted. He seemed like he was almost shy about calling Rayne's friend. Was it possible that Jason the ultimate playboy was interested in a relationship with someone and not multiple someones?

"Well, yeah, she's getting a settlement, but it's not like the money matters to me. You know that, I'm set. But I am glad she will have something to rely on. She doesn't have any family and only a few friends. So yeah, this will be good for her," Walt said.

"If she is what makes you happy, then I'm happy for you, man." Jason held out his hand for a fist bump. "Is she the one that Zak hung that goofy wind chime for?"

"Heard about that, did you? Yes, she is," Walt said softly. She was the one he would do a lot of things for, if she would let him.

Walt got to work going through some of the inventory lists and things. Not that he didn't trust Jason; he just liked to know where they were at on things. After he had been working for a while, his phone chimed with a text and he pulled it out of his pocket. It was a text from his housekeeper.

I needed to go out anyway, so it was no big deal. I stopped by and threw your dinner in the oven. It will be ready by 5:30. And may I suggest that you have dinner in the dining room tonight. I know you don't use it often, but it might be a good setting for this evening.

She had ended it with a smiley and a winking emoji. Walt wasn't sure what his housekeeper had gotten herself up to, but he was pretty sure he was going to owe her a bonus and a thank you by the time the evening was done.

Walt noticed that Jason was talking to Rayne, but not with his usual flirtatiousness. He seemed to just be chatting and making sure that she was okay. He refilled her drink a couple of times and just kind of kept an eye on her while he was doing his other duties and taking care of other customers. When it was time for him to leave, he called Jason into the office.

"Look, man," he said, putting his hand out for a handshake. "I'm sorry about earlier, I was being a possessive asshole. I know you wouldn't try to steal my girl."

Jason shook his hand and said, "Oh, I would totally try to take your girl, if I thought she was just some girl you were banging." He laughed. "But, nah man, I can tell you really care about this one. I'll never try to overstep, and I'll do anything I can to help if you need me."

Walt knew that was true. Despite his playboy ways and his rarely serious attitude, Jason was one of the good guys. Walt walked out to the bar and sat by Rayne. Jason came back over so Walt asked, "Did my friend here take good care of you, sweetheart?"

"Yes, he's been a great host. Well, other than all the questions he asked," she teased. Was Jason's face getting red?

"Questions? What have you been grilling my girl about, Jase?" Walt asked.

It was obvious that Jason didn't want to answer, so Rayne piped in with, "Oh, he just wanted to know a little about Sunni, that's all. No big deal." And yep, there it was; Jason's face got even more red.

Walt decided not to give his friend a hard time. He just looked at him and smiled. "Well, I'm done here if you're ready to head home." He held out his elbow for her to take and they walked out together.

Chapter Seventeen

When they got to Walt's house and opened the door, the smell coming from the oven was heavenly. Rayne looked at him questioningly. "Uh, Mrs. Steele texted me that she had been in the area, so she stopped by to put something in the oven for your homecoming meal," Walt explained. "I think she missed you too."

"But I've never met her," Rayne protested.

"No, but she saw the effects. Dishes were actually in the dishwasher, not piling up in the sink." He shrugged. "What can I say? You have a good effect on me."

Walt found the note on the counter that told him the directions for putting the rest of the meal on the table. He went into the dining room and it was confirmed: he owed Mrs. Steele a bonus. There were candles on the table with a vase of beautiful flowers. The places were all set with his best china, which he almost never used but had bought just in case. It was set up for a night of romance and celebration. There was champagne chilling in the wine fridge along with several other choices for wine if champagne wasn't Rayne's thing.

Rayne walked into the room trying to find out where Walt had gone. "Wow, I guess she was happy I was coming back," Rayne said. She looked impressed by the gorgeous table.

"I think she got wind of it being a celebration of sorts," Walt remarked.

"Ah, okay then, what can I do to help?" Rayne asked.

"Nothing, sweetheart. It's pretty much done other than taking things out of the oven and putting things on the table."

"Well, I can help with that then," Rayne said determinedly and headed back into the kitchen.

Yep, no one could ever say his girl was a slacker. He joined her in the kitchen and started warming the last few things on the list. Rayne helped get dishes to the table and soon they were ready to sit down and eat. For some reason, Walt was a little nervous. He really wanted tonight to go well. He would take it as fast or as slow as Rayne wanted him to; it didn't even matter if they had sex tonight. He just wanted to get their relationship moving in the right direction.

They didn't talk a lot at dinner, some pleasant conversation, but they also seemed comfortable with times of silence. *This is how things should be with a couple*, Rayne thought. She loved being here with Walt. She was starting to hope that maybe they did have a long-term future. After dinner was over, they cleared the table together and then Walt grabbed their wine glasses and the rest of the bottle and headed for the living room. When they got to the living room, Rayne couldn't believe her eyes. Her pictures were there, on display, photos of her parents and of her and Sunni. She turned all the way around, noticing how many of her things had found their way onto Walt's shelves.

"Why did you do this?" Rayne asked.

Walt wasn't sure if she was upset about it, or okay with it from the sound of her voice, so he tried to think of the answer that wouldn't upset her more. "Oh, uh, well, I saw your box that said photos on it, and I opened it. I'm sorry; you don't have to leave them out here if you don't want to. I wasn't trying to invade your privacy, I promise. I just thought that if you were going to be here you might like a few of your things around. I really do have lots of space for it all." He ran his hands through his hair. Maybe he had really screwed up. He hoped not. "Look, I'm sorry. I obviously overstepped." He reached for one of the pictures he had placed on the mantle to take it down to give to her, but she stopped him.

There were tears in her eyes. "No, Walt, you don't understand, I'm not upset, I'm overwhelmed. You have given me so much and the way you try to make sure I feel welcome in your home is beyond anything I could have hoped for," she assured him. "Just giving me a room that was on the first floor was so sweet of you but trying to make sure that I felt at home here is, it's... well, it's just.... wow. I don't even have words." She wrapped her arms around him and buried her face in his chest. He held her tightly. He would hold her for as long as she needed him to. Rayne pulled away several minutes later, but not out of his arms, just enough that she could look him in the eye. What she saw there made her heart feel so light. He really did care about her happiness. No one had done that in a long time other than Sunni.

Walt continued to hold on to her as she stared into his eyes. Yep, he was in it up to his eyeballs with this woman. He leaned in to kiss her and she eagerly responded. Walt did not want to take this too fast, but his body was having other ideas. He pulled back before he got too carried away. He put one hand on each side of her face and looked deep into her eyes as he said, "Look, sweetheart, there is nothing more than I would rather do than take you upstairs to my bed. But I will be as patient as you need me to be, Rayne. I'm just putting this out there. It doesn't have to be tonight. Or if you want to go upstairs and just make out some more, I will be okay with that. I am not going to pressure you into doing anything you don't want to do."

And she knew immediately that he wouldn't. He would be a gentleman and they would go only as far as she was comfortable going. She was pretty sure she wanted to go all the way. But she knew that if things got to be too much and she asked him to stop, he would.

"Yes, Walt," she said softly. "I want to go upstairs. As far as the rest, can we just play it by ear since it's my first time?"

Walt smiled. "I'm totally fine with that, sweetheart." He bent and before Rayne knew it, she was in his arms being carried up the stairs. He promised her a tour of the entire upstairs later. But for now, he took her to the huge master bedroom at the end of the hall. He placed her gently on the bed and took off his tie. He tossed that aside and started to unbutton his shirt. Rayne had seen him without a shirt while swimming, and she knew he was built. This was different. As he was undressing, it was like he was revealing himself to her slowly in a way she had never seen before. As he unbuttoned his shirt, she could see just how ripped he really was. Each abdominal muscle was its own separate ridge on his torso. She could see the V of muscle that started downward to his pants. This man was obviously someone who worked out, like a lot. She hadn't ever seen him do anything more than swim, but it was obvious he did more than that somewhere. Her mouth was watering by the time his shirt hit the floor. He crawled onto the bed and leaned over her and they started kissing again.

"If you want me to stop, or slow down at any time, just say so," he assured her before taking her lips again.

Rayne was pretty sure she wouldn't want him to stop, not ever, but slowing down, she wasn't sure. As wonderful as all of this was feeling, it was a little overwhelming too.

He began kissing her again, deep kisses, his tongue doing a dance with hers. It was making her get very very warm in all sorts of places and ways. He started kissing his way down her neck toward her chest, and it was then that she remembered that she wasn't wearing any sexy underwear or anything, mostly because she didn't own any. Dancers tended to need more 'practical' undergarments. Oh well, she couldn't worry about that now, but she saw a shopping trip with Sunni in her near future. Like, tomorrow would be good.

Walt started to unbutton the buttons on her blouse. He went slowly and kissed each expanse of skin that he uncovered. He was going slowly; he wanted this so badly, but he vowed that he would make it good for her even if it gave him blue balls before she was ready. He parted her shirt when he got to the bottom. She seemed to be trying to cover herself a little bit and he was afraid that she was getting cold feet.

"Is something wrong, sweetheart?" he asked.

"Um, just that I know that my bra isn't very sexy," she said.

Well, if that was all that caused her hesitation, he could handle that. "It's fine, sweetheart, I would be more surprised if you were dressed in what most people consider sexy. I know you aren't experienced, baby. I'm not expecting anything more from you than you have to give." He unhooked the front hook on her bra and leaned back a bit to look at her. "Now, that is gorgeous," Walt breathed before leaning in to kiss her breasts. He lavished attention on each one in turn. Avoiding the nipple for now. He just wanted to worship her body and let her know just how sexy she was to him.

Rayne was squirming under all this attention; she knew she wanted more of what Walt was doing and she wanted him to do more than he was, but her brain was sort of in a fog with how good all of this was feeling. She realized that Walt was saying something and from the way he was saying it, it wasn't the first time he had tried to get her attention.

She pulled herself out of the euphoric fog she found herself in and looked up at him. "Sorry, what?" She sounded a little drunk to her own ears.

Walt gave her a big smile. "Nothing to be sorry about, baby. I just wanted you to lean up so that I could take these the rest of the way off. And your slacks too, if that's okay with you."

She nodded and sat up enough that he could get the clothing off her upper body then lay back and raised her hips so he could take her pants off. She lay there in her light pink panties, again, nothing sexy, but Walt didn't seem to mind. He went right back to kissing her chest, breasts and stomach before starting to work his way down further. She felt like she was going to implode. He skipped past her panties and started kissing his way up her legs, to her thighs. She didn't have enough experience to be able to say for sure, but she was pretty sure Walt was trying to torture her by doing all this kissing and nothing else. She was also pretty sure that Walt knew exactly how to seduce a woman. That thought didn't bother her; he was six years older than her. He had been a frat boy and was now a successful attorney and co-owner of a bar. Not to mention drop-dead gorgeous. Of course women had probably thrown themselves at him. She wasn't jealous; she was kind of glad that she was with a man who knew what he was doing. She would hate to think how bad it would be to be with someone who knew as little as she did about sex. She was sure it wouldn't be anywhere near as enjoyable as this was turning out to be.

Walt kissed her legs and her inner thighs. He kept looking up to make sure that Rayne's eyes were still closed and that she seemed to be enjoying what was happening. He was watching closely for any sign of discomfort or fear on her face. He saw none. So he kissed the edges of her panties, again watching her face for reaction. She took a deep inhale and her hips raised up slightly like she was trying to get more. He moved them to the side so he could kiss the plump flesh at the sides of her mound. She just kept squirming and breathing hard. Her eyes remained closed. Walt leaned up so that he could get the waistband of her panties and started to pull them down, kissing her as he went. He moved slowly, giving her every chance to ask him to slow down if she needed him to. When he got the panties down around her ankles, she lifted her feet so that he could take them off completely.

He put his face back above her pussy and then he looked up at her and asked, "Are we still doing okay here, sweetheart?"

"Um-hmmm," she moaned.

Walt lowered his face and began licking and kissing at her sweet pussy, He gave gentle little nips with his teeth to see how she would respond to that. She kept moaning and moving her hips, pressing herself up toward him if he pulled back a little. He guessed his girl was enjoying herself. He used his fingers to part her labia so that he could lick at her pussy and circle her clit with his tongue. He found her to be very wet. That was what he was hoping for. It looked like his girl was going to be good to go when he got there. He cautioned himself to be prepared for the fact that she still could back out. And, if she did, that would be okay. He would hold her and hopefully sleep with her in his arms all night.

Walt inserted his middle finger into her and began slowly moving it in and out. She was so tight; he knew he was going to have to take this slow and easy. Rayne kept rocking her body to the rhythm that Walt was setting with his fingers. He could tell she was enjoying his actions very much, so he inserted another finger and then gradually added a third. He realized that he needed to give her at least one, maybe two orgasms before he even tried to put his cock in her. He needed her to be very wet and very aroused before he pursued his own pleasure. He knew once he got inside her, he wouldn't last long. She would be like a vise around him.

He needed to see her face and watch her reactions, so he moved up to kiss her, his thumb taking over where his mouth had been. He didn't slow the rhythm of his fingers; he kept thrusting them in and out at a steady pace while his thumb made circles around her clit. He kissed her lips deeply, sucking her lower lip into his mouth for a gentle nip. She was really getting into this. She was kissing him as passionately as he was kissing her. Her body began to thrash even more than she had been, and Walt knew she must be close. Proving him correct, she tensed up and then an orgasm was rolling through her whole body.

Rayne had officially just had her mind blown. Nothing had ever felt that amazing in her life. Now she understood why people referred to it as "the big O." It was big, all right; her whole body had felt the ripple from that orgasm. She wanted to make Walt feel as good as he had just made her feel, but she felt so inept at this, she had no idea what she should do. She had read a few books with these type of scenes in them, but she had never actually done anything. After her mind cleared a bit, she realized that Walt was just lying beside her, half dressed, looking down at her face. She wondered if she had said or done something wrong, although she didn't know how that would be possible since she had just basically gone along for the ride.

****

"You're beautiful when you come for me, Rayne." Walt was looking deep into her eyes when he said that. So, nothing wrong then. She must have been okay if he would say something like that. She had never had anyone who made her feel as beautiful as Walt did, other than her parents, and parents were kind of obligated to like how their kid looked. She had always felt beautiful when she danced ballet, but obviously Walt liked the way she looked even though ballet wasn't in her future anymore. She smiled up at him and then she asked, "Do I get to see how beautiful you are? You haven't even taken off all your clothes and I am lying here completely exposed."

"Ah, well, first of all," Walt said with a bit of a glint in his eye, "there may be times when I just enjoy looking at how beautiful you are. But before I take my clothes off, I need to know just how far you want this to go tonight. If you don't want to go any further than we already have, that is totally fine. I will change into some pajama pants and lay here beside you holding you all night. I want you to understand that, Rayne. I would be content to just have you sleep in my arms. We can take this as fast or as slow as you want it to go."

Wow, this guy was saying all the right things to make her fall for him even more. But what could she say without sounding like a total loser? Yes, she wanted to continue, she wanted to eventually make love to him, but she had absolutely no clue where to go from here or what to do next. She wanted to make him feel amazing, just like he had for her, but she didn't know the first step toward making that happen.

Apparently, she was thinking too hard and too long because Walt started to pull away to get up. "Rayne, it really is okay. We don't have to go any further," he assured her as he started to get up off the bed. "I do hope you will sleep up here with me tonight, though. I can go get you some night clothes, or you can wear one of my T-shirts, or whatever makes you feel the most comfortable."

He was standing by the bed, waiting for her answer. She just didn't know how to say it. But she had to try. So she stammered out her best effort at saying what she really wanted. "No, Walt, wait, um, I mean, I don't know how to say what's in my head right now, I... I've never, um done anything like this before."

"I know that, sweetheart, and that's totally fine. We don't have to go any further than you are comfortable with." Again, with the reassurances, Walt knew how to make her feel very at ease with him, which was exactly why she wanted him to be the one to take her virginity. He wasn't just going to push her into something she wasn't ready for. He was willing to wait however long it would take for her to be ready, but the thing was, she was ready now. She just didn't know how to say it. Walt started to turn away to go do whatever it was he needed to do before going to sleep. She realized that he really was exactly who she wanted to do this with for her first time. "Walt, what I mean is, I do want to do this, I mean, I want to make love or have sex or whatever you want to call it. I want to do this with you."

During her rambled sentence, Walt had turned back around and was facing her again. He sat on the edge of the bed and stroked his finger down her cheek, brushing a lock of her hair off her face. He looked into her eyes, like he was trying to see her very soul. Most likely he was trying to be sure that she really meant what she had said. She was in so deep with this man, but that didn't feel like a bad thing; in fact, it felt like a really good thing.

She had to make him believe that she really did want this with him, so she tried again. "I realize that I am probably saying this all wrong, but I do want to continue, I do want this, I want you to teach me how to make you feel as good as you have made me feel tonight. I want you to make love to me." There, she couldn't have said it any more plainly than that.

Walt was still looking deeply into her eyes, but his smile started to grow. "Sweetheart, tonight, all I want to do is make you feel good and make love to you if that's what you want. That will make me feel everything. I don't need you to do anything to me or for me, just let me make love to you. We can explore other things later or another day, but tonight, I just want to make love to you and sleep with you in my arms."

"That's what I want too," she said softly, but still with conviction. No more hesitation, she knew she wanted to go forward with this night.

Walt stood up and started working on the rest of his clothing. While he undressed, he was saying things about how if she wanted to stop at any time, that was fine, and he would be as gentle as he could. He was saying lots of things, but not many of them really registered because he was undressing, and this was the first time she had ever seen a man this gorgeous getting naked. Sure, she had seen pictures, girls at the dance studio always had pictures of the latest Hollywood heartthrob or some male model wearing little clothing. This was different; this was a real man, one she could touch and kiss and look at in depth. Wow, this man was fit. He had more than a six-pack. His was more like an eight-pack of well-defined muscle. There was just the right amount of hair on his chest. Rayne had never liked hairy men in the pictures, but she also hadn't found the ones of men who had no chest hair all that appealing either. Walt had just enough to look masculine and sexy without going overboard and looking like a relative of Sasquatch. But that chest had absolutely no comparison to the rest of the man. When he pulled his pants down, his legs were like chiseled marble, muscles that made it obvious that he worked out quite regularly, but they didn't look like he was trying to be some musclebound show-off. He just looked very masculine and very sexy—to Rayne, anyway.

She also liked the fact that he wore boxer briefs. She had seen enough men's underwear ads to know that she didn't like actual boxers, too baggy and hid the deliciousness that was underneath, but she also didn't like the "tight whiteys." Those made her think of her father too much, since that had been what he had worn. She had helped with the laundry after her mother had died.

But boxer briefs, those she liked. And this man could fill out a pair of them perfectly. She could see his well-sculpted ass filling out the back while he had turned to put his pants over the chest at the foot of the bed. But when he turned back and walked back toward her on the bed, she could see the evidence of the one part of a man she had never seen before, in pictures or in real life. She was almost anxious for him to take those boxer briefs off so she could see all of him. But he kept them on when he lay on the bed beside her again. She must have had a disappointed look on her face because he sorts of chuckled when he said, "We'll get to that in a minute, but first I want to say a couple of things. I really did mean it when I said, we could still stop at any time, if anything hurts—no, wait, I can't say that. I am pretty sure there is going to be a bit of pain, there always is the first time. So, let's just say this: if something is too uncomfortable or is beyond what you are okay with, say so, and we'll stop, immediately. I also want you to know that I haven't had sex with anyone since my last physical and I am totally clean, but we will use condoms anyway because I am pretty sure that you aren't on any method of birth control." He looked at her and she shook her head to confirm that he was right, she wasn't on any birth control because she had never had a reason to be before. "Right, then, that is something we can talk about as we go forward with this relationship, if we want to use condoms or if another method would be something we want to try."

Rayne liked that he had referred to it as a relationship; that reassured her that he was having at least some of the same feelings she was about this not just being some one-night stand or something cheap and tawdry. He was acknowledging that there was something between them and they were going to go forward and see where that might go. She wasn't thinking marriage or anything like that—it was way too soon—but to know that he was invested in this too gave her a special feeling in her heart. Walt leaned down and started kissing her again, and she realized that even the time their bodies had been apart, and talking about birth control really hadn't done much to take away the amazing feelings her body had experienced. As soon as he kissed her, she could feel her body heating up toward that peak again. Shouldn't he be taking off his underwear by now? She really wanted to see all of him.

She said, "Aren't you going to take your boxers off?"

Walt just smiled and said, "Soon, but if I let myself I would rush this way too much, and this first time for you has to go a little slower."

Walt wanted nothing more than to tear his underwear off and be on top of her and her question just about pushed him over that edge. But he knew he had to maintain his control. He had never actually taken someone's virginity before, but he had heard enough stories and learned from books basically what it was like for the woman. He knew there was pretty much a guarantee that there would be some pain involved, but he was going to do his best to make that something that was quick and hopefully minor. A guy could hope, anyway. At the very least, he was going to make sure she was wet and ready for him again before any penetration would happen.

Walt began kissing her lips and then moved down her neck, kissing the soft flesh behind her ear. Rayne moaned softly. *Ah, another sweet spot*, Walt thought to himself. He was making mental notes of her reactions. He nipped lightly at her neck and she just squirmed and asked for more. Walt could do that; he could give her more and more and more.

He dragged his teeth across her shoulder and then traced that same path back to her neck using his tongue to soothe the small bit of pain his teeth had most likely caused. She just moaned more. She was tangling her hands in his hair as if she needed something to hold on to to ground her to earth. He kissed a trail to her breast and again gently bit on the extended nipple. He alternated small bites and sucking on each nipple in turn. Every time he bit down, Rayne moaned even louder. He began stroking her clit again while still giving her nipples lots of attention. He could tell she was already close to another orgasm. He inserted two fingers inside her and with his other hand began fondling her other nipple. As he pinched down harder than he had before, he looked into her eyes and with a commanding voice said, "Come for me, Rayne. Come hard and long."

And she did. She couldn't help it. Rayne felt like there were a million electrical circuits running through every part of her body and every single one of them had lit up at once. She heard herself calling out Walt's name and begging for more, but it almost seemed like it was more something she heard rather than mentally telling herself to do it. This was such an amazing feeling. Walt had stretched himself out beside her on the bed, and somehow, he had gotten his boxers off and a condom on. She did not remember how that had happened. Walt told her to get up on her knees and straddle him. Her brain was still a little foggy from the mind-blowing orgasm he had just given her, so she was slow to move, but move she did. She was finally going to get to see what it felt like to be fully with a man. She would know what all the hype was about when her classmates and peers had giggled and carried on and on when they talked about sex. When she was on her knees straddling him, she could feel his hard cock pressed against her. She couldn't wait to see what it felt like when it was inside her.

Walt put a hand on each of her hips and looked into her eyes. "Okay, Rayne, full disclosure here. I have never taken anyone's virginity before, but I have talked to people who have. There will most likely be at least a little bit of pain involved. Unfortunately, there isn't anything that can be done about that. But hopefully I can help minimize that as much as possible, and hopefully it will be brief. Now, I am going to lift you up off me and I want you to use your hand to line me up with you so that just the tip is inside of you. And, if at any time it gets to be too much, just say so and I will stop. I promise, I don't care what stage we are at, we will stop if you need to."

God, he hoped she didn't want to stop, he was so ready for this. But he would keep his word and stop somehow, if Rayne needed him to. Rayne obeyed his instructions to the letter, although he almost embarrassed himself like a horny little schoolboy when he felt her wrap her hand around the base of his dick. But he controlled himself. He almost lost it again when she inserted the tip into her wet slick pussy. But again, his mind was able to get his body back under control. When she was fully on top of him and his dick was lined up correctly, he told her, "Now, let me control this for the first few minutes. I will do my best to make it quick."

Rayne nodded her agreement to his directions. Walt moved her up and down on his cock, trying to go a little deeper with each up and down. When he felt his dick hit up against resistance, he knew he was there. It was time to make this happen. The next time he pulled her down, he also thrust his hips up and then just held them there for a while. He heard the sharp intake of breath when he felt that resistance give way inside her. He just held her there, his thumbs making slow circles on her hips to try to soothe her in some way.

He was probably the biggest bastard on the planet at that point in time, because even though he knew it had caused her some pain, he was feeling higher than a kite about being inside her finally. He knew he really hadn't known her very long, but it had still felt like he was waiting forever when he would hold her in his arms and dance or kiss her but not be able to go any further at the time. But now, finally, he was where he had wanted to be for weeks. He loosened his hold on her hips so that she could decide what happened next. She started to move up and down of her own volition and Walt silently thanked whatever god or good fortune had smiled on him and given him this beautiful woman. He also realized that he was going to come far too quickly, so he needed to make sure she was ready to go over that cliff again, hopefully right in sync with him this time.

Rayne had felt that sharp pain, but it really had been brief. But she was also realizing how good it had felt to have him move her up and down on his stiff cock. When he moved his hands off her hips, she started to mimic the way he had been moving her. She felt full of how large his cock was but she also felt sensations like she had never known before. She also tried to rotate her hips a little so she was moving on him in a different way. With the fact that she wasn't up to her full strength, she wasn't able to rock and rotate the way she really wanted to. This felt like heaven to her. Walt put his hand between them, and she felt his thumb seek out her clit.

He started rubbing circles and pressing firmly. It started that same feeling she had had earlier; she knew that another orgasm was building deep inside her. When she started moving faster, he pressed harder on her clit and made faster circles. She was about to lose it again. She heard Walt say something about 'going together' just before she went over that cliff for the third time this evening. She felt the sensation of Walt's orgasm pulsing in her at almost the same time.

She collapsed onto Walt's muscular chest and tried to catch her breath. "That was..." She trailed off. She didn't know what word to use: amazing, awesome, mind blowing, all of them fit. Walt just seemed to agree, even though she hadn't fully finished her sentence. He made an "um-hmm" sound that she felt more than heard, with her head so close to his heart. She could hear that his heartbeat was going rapidly, but then again, so was hers.

Walt allowed Rayne to stay lying on top of him while they both caught their breath and slowed the beating of their hearts, but he knew he didn't dare let her stay that way very long. His cock was already starting to react to the fact that she was still straddling him. And as much as he would love to make love to her again, he knew she was already most likely going to feel some tenderness in the morning. He didn't need to be a Neanderthal and make it worse on her.

He cradled her to him as he rolled them both to their sides, facing each other. Rayne looked beautiful, but she also looked kind of worn out. She mumbled a soft "Thank you" and gave him the most beautiful smile he had ever seen.

"You never have to thank me for sex, sweetheart. I am pretty sure I enjoyed that even more than you did." He rolled away from her to dispose of the condom in the trash by his bed and that was when he noticed the small amount of blood on him. Yep, he knew that was likely to happen too. He stood up and started toward the master bathroom. Rayne started to protest, but he turned to her and assured her that he would be right back. He started to fill the big tub before grabbing a washcloth to clean himself. When the tub was full, he walked back out to the bed. Rayne was falling asleep fast, so he scooped her up into his arms and walked her to the bathtub.

"I do know how to walk, you know," Rayne protested.

"I know you do, but this gives me an excuse to hold you." Walt could still smell the soft fragrance of her hair. He made a note to himself that tomorrow, they needed to move all her things upstairs. That was if she was ready to share a room with him. If she wasn't ready, that was okay. The first floor would be easier for her to maneuver on her own, and she would still be in his home. He would just have to work harder to win her over so she would be willing to share a room with him. He deposited her gently into the tub of warm water. Rayne re-positioned herself and her eyes went wide. "This tub is even bigger than the one in my room—err, I mean the guest room."

Walt knew he needed to 'start as you intend to go,' as his mother had always told him. "No, Rayne, you were right the first time. It has been your room, and you have every right to call it that. I offered it to you for as long as you need it. I am kind of hoping that it becomes the guest room again soon, though."

Rayne sat up abruptly. "Oh, yes, of course, I am sure you need it for other guests you may want to have over. I am sure I can manage my own apartment. I don't need to keep tying up your spare room."

Walt sat on the edge of the tub and put a finger over her lip to stop her from talking anymore. "First of all, Rayne, this house has five bedrooms and 5 and a half baths. So if I were expecting any other guests, which I'm not, by the way, you wouldn't have to give up your first-floor room to anyone. What I was hoping was that maybe you would consider moving up here, to my room. I would really like to sleep with you every night. Unless you think the stairs are going to be a problem. I can help you when I am here, but if you don't feel you can handle them when you might be here alone, I will completely understand if you want to stay on the main floor. If you feel more comfortable on the main floor but are still willing to spend your nights with me, I can sleep down there. Whatever works best for you. Honestly, I am open to whatever makes you feel most comfortable." He tapped her nose with his finger and assured her that she didn't have to make the decision right now. "Why don't you think on it and I will go downstairs and lock up and shut the lights off for the night. Whatever you decide will be okay with me."

Rayne objected, "Well, at least let me pay rent or something to help out. Lord knows I can afford it now. Thanks to you and my millions."

Walt just chuckled at that and shook his head as he walked out of the room. Rayne started weighing the pros and the cons of moving in with him as in really with him, not just as a guest. Did she want to sleep with him and see where this relationship might go? That was a resounding "HELL YES!!!" Could she handle the stairs if Walt wasn't here to help her? That was another 'yes'. She might go slowly but, he had handrails, so it wouldn't be a problem. Besides, the bed in her room was most likely a queen. The one in his room had been massive, most likely one of those California kings she had heard about. Walt wasn't a huge guy, but he was big enough. Probably 6' 2" or so compared to her 5' 5". So the bed would be more comfortable for him if they stayed in his room. Her mind then drifted to the settlement she was going to be getting. She really wanted to do something special for Walt with that money. She knew the law firm was getting a share, but she also knew that Walt had said he wasn't going to take his cut from it because he wanted her to have more. So if she couldn't pay rent, and he wouldn't take his fee, she had to figure out some way to do something nice for him; after all, she was getting over thirteen million dollars after the law firm got their pay. She wasn't even sure just how many commas were in a number that big. She had never had any reason to care before.

She let out a squeal of joy—not a loud one; she didn't want Walt to come running, but a squeal nonetheless—and then sank deeper into the water so that all that was out of the water was her head. This tub really was massive, way bigger than the one downstairs. This one could easily hold two people. That got her mind going on just what she and Walt might be able to do in this huge tub. She apparently had had a sex fiend buried deep inside her and now Walt had unlocked the cage, because she was starting to think of all sorts of things that might be fun to try with Walt.

Walt made his usual nightly rounds, checking doors and windows, turning off lights. He was thinking about the comment Rayne had made. Let her pay rent? Like he would ever take money from his girlfriend to help with expenses in his home. He was thinking about that very thing when an idea came to his mind. He looked at his watch and realized it wasn't late, so he picked up the phone and made a call.

When Susan answered with a bright, "Hello, Walt, what can I do for you? Are you finally ready to sell that gorgeous home of yours and you're going to give me the commission?" Walt smiled at her enthusiasm, but went on to tell her, "Sorry to disappoint you, Susan. I like this house too much to leave it for now anyway, But I might have a way that you can earn a decent commission on another sale."

He could tell he had piqued her interest when all she said was "Oh?"

He went on to explain, "I have a friend who may be looking for a commercial building. It must be in a good neighborhood but have easy access to bus lines. It must be big, preferably with large open floor plans. But if the structure would be up to it, it wouldn't be a huge issue to remodel it. I don't have a set price in mind, but the space must be worth the price tag. If you know what I mean."

"Yeah, yeah, I think I got you. Want to clue me in on what this building is going to be used for? It might help me narrow my search," Susan asked.

"Yeah, think dance studio," Walt replied.

"Why, Walt, do you have a secret dance instructor hidden in there somewhere?" Susan joked.

"No, but I know a beautiful dancer that I am hoping might be open to the idea of starting her own dance school. So let me know if you find anything and I will look at it before I show it to her. I still have to sell the whole plan." And as he said it, he realized that really was most likely to be the biggest hurdle to jump in his plan. Rayne might not want to teach dance if she couldn't be a dancer herself.

"I'm on it," Susan said. "I'll let you know what I find. Thanks for thinking of me on this one, Walt. It's not my usual transaction, but I could definitely use the commission on a big sale like that."

"No problem, Susan. Good night." Walt hung up his phone and pretty much jogged up the steps. He needed to get back to his girl and he needed to start to figure out ways to start nudging her toward the goal of owning her own dance school.

When Walt walked back into the bathroom, he was only wearing his boxer briefs. He must have slipped them back on before he went downstairs. Rayne started to pout and object to the fact that he had clothes and she didn't. She firmly believed they should be equally naked. But then she noticed that he had grabbed her big fluffy robe from the guest room downstairs, so her protest died on her lips. Besides, she had come to a conclusion while he had been gone. She needed to tell him about it.

"So I was thinking that since I am going to be getting all this money, I know one thing that I would really like to buy for myself." She could tell her excitement must have shown on her face because Walt had a big grin on his face when he asked her what she was going to be spending the money on. "I want a car, a nice car. I've never had one before other than the junker that my dad left to me when he died."

At first, saying that phrase started to bring back the hurt she had always felt over losing her dad, but she fought it back. This was something to be happy about, and she was going to start moving forward. She wasn't exactly sure where she was going just yet, but she had to start thinking about a future and with Walt in the picture, at least for the time being, it was looking bright.

Chapter Eighteen

When Rayne woke up the next morning, she realized that Walt wasn't in bed with her anymore, so she looked around the room just in time to see him coming out of his walk-in closet.

"Ah, good, you're awake. I need to go in to work for a few hours and I didn't want to just leave a note if I could help it." Walt was smiling like he was happy to have some time with her. "I need to drop by the office for a few hours to make sure everything is filed and closed on your case and make sure nothing new has come up, which will most likely be boring as hell, but I have my afternoon free. I was thinking maybe I could pick you up for lunch about 1 o'clock and we could go look at some cars."

Rayne started to object, but Walt put a finger to her lips to shush her. "I know what you're going to say. You don't have the money yet, but trust me, sweetheart, with the paperwork I have any dealership will be happy to work with you."

Walt leaned over and kissed her, and she eagerly responded, putting her arms around him to try to pull him closer. He had given her one of his T-shirts to sleep in and he had slept in his boxer briefs. Now, he was fully dressed in what had to be a tailored suit. It fit him perfectly. And she had to admit, he looked delicious fully clothed or barely dressed.

Walt pulled away from the kiss just enough to be able to give her a stern look. "As much as I would love to continue what you are trying to get started," he said with a devilish look, "I really do have to go do these depositions. I made breakfast. Yours is in the warming oven and Mrs. Steele should be here around 9. She knows that you are here, and I want you to feel free to add anything you want to her shopping list. If there are foods you want to have on hand, just tell her what they are." Walt leaned over and kissed her again, then pulled himself away. "And, on that note, I have to go. Can't be late or Dddy will grumble," he said with a chuckle as he walked out the door. He peeked back in and added, "Feel free to use anything you find around; you can use the computer in my office if you want to do any research on cars or whatever. See you at one." With that, he turned around and was gone. Rayne looked at the clock on the nightstand and realized it was already 8 o'clock. If she was going to be presentable for Mrs. Steele, she had better get her butt out of bed.

She started to walk into Walt's bathroom, but she realized that all her clothes and toiletries were still downstairs. She went to what had become her room and sat on the bed, looking at all the ways Walt had really made this into a room for her. All the subtle rainbows in paintings and on the bedding, it was all picked out with care specifically for her. Unless Sunni had something to do with it. She picked up her phone, which had been left on the charger in her room. When Sunni answered, she immediately started the inquisition. "Did you help Walt pick out that wind-chime and the décor of this room?"

Sunni laughed a little and then said "Good morning to you too, Rayne. It's so good to hear from you."

Rayne realized that she had most likely come across as a woman obsessed and she apologized. "Sorry, Sunni, good morning. I didn't mean to come across so rudely, but I need to know just how much you had to do with all of these things."

"Well, he asked me if there was anything that you liked or collected because your room at the rehab was so plain, he wanted to try to brighten it up for you," Sunni said. "But that was the extent of anything I have had to do with it. He asked, I answered, and then he did the rest all on his own."

"Wow," Rayne said.

"Yeah, wow," Sunni agreed. "I hope I can find a man that cares for me as much as Walt cares about you someday."

"And, on a totally different note, Walt asked me to move upstairs into his room last night," Rayne said.

"And did you?" Sunni asked and then she let out what sounded a lot like a squeal and asked, "Oh my God, Rayne did you?" Her voice suggested that she was no longer asking about the move upstairs as much as she was asking about something totally different.

"Well, no, I have not moved upstairs. My things are all still in the room on the first floor. But I think I am going to move up there. And as to the other implication, yes, I did," Rayne said shyly.

"Oh my God, oh, my God," Sunni said, and it sounded like she might be jumping up and down on the other end of the line. "You aren't a virgin anymore. Was it painful? Was it amazing? Spill the details, girlfriend."

"Well, there was a little pain, of course, but Walt absolutely knew what he was doing. It was like two seconds and then it was gone again, and the rest was definitely amazing," Rayne assured her. "Maybe we can get together for lunch some day later this week or something and talk about it. I still need to get dressed for the day. Apparently, the housekeeper will be here at 9 and I am supposed to tell her if I want things added to the shopping list or anything. I don't know how to handle this, Sunni. I've never had a housekeeper before. This seems surreal."

"Just enjoy it, Rayne," Sunni assured her. "I'm sure Walt pays her very well and if he wants you to be able to have her do things for you, then go for it. Tell her what things you would like added. Make sure you tell her to buy lots of chocolate for when I come over." Sunni laughed. "I have to get going too. I have a client in a bit. Not all of us can sit back and live on our millions."

Rayne knew that her friend wasn't jealous—well, maybe she was a bit jealous, who wouldn't be? But she wasn't being malicious about it. She was just teasing, so Rayne played along. "Yes, you should go to work and I will sit here and prepare for the housekeeper and then I am going to surf the net to decide what kind of car I want to buy." Rayne paused for a minute, and then added, "How silly is that? I am getting all this money and I have no clue what to do with it other than knowing that I want a car. I don't think I will be spending millions on a car, but at least I have the money to buy whatever one I want."

"I'm happy for you, girly," Sunni replied. "Go out there and get your dream car. We'll talk later."

"Right, bye, Sunni," Rayne said. "And, thanks for the part you played in helping Walt and me to get together. I don't know where it will go, but, for right now, it feels pretty good."

"You deserve it, Rayne. Talk to you later." And with that, Sunni hung up the phone.

Rayne realized her time was slipping by and she was still just sitting there in Walt's T-shirt. Wouldn't that be a great way to meet the housekeeper for the first time? She decided to skip a shower; after all, she had washed up in Walt's humongous tub last night. She hadn't washed her hair because she didn't have her own products upstairs, but it still looked okay. She decided on a pantsuit that would be comfortable enough for car shopping, but most likely let her fit in wherever it was that Walt was taking her for lunch. He was in a suit also, so it should be fine. After getting dressed, she went and found the most delicious looking waffle she had ever seen in the warming oven next to it sat a bowl of strawberry compote to put on the waffle. This man was spoiling her.

She was sitting at the breakfast nook enjoying her waffle when an older woman came in the back door. She wasn't old, just older, Rayne figured; maybe in her 50s or so.

"You must be Mrs. Steele," Rayne said at the same time that the woman said, "You must be Rayne." They were both holding their hands out to each other and both laughed a little at the fact that they had basically said the same thing at the same time.

"Well, I am pleased to meet you," Mrs. Steele continued. "It's so wonderful to see Walt have someone to spend time with other than his buddies at that bar. Not that the bar is a bad thing," she was quick to clarify. "But it's nice to see him interested in a woman, if you know what I mean." She gave Rayne a little wink.

"Well, I'm sure I'm not the first woman he has had here with him," Rayne protested.

"Actually, you would be," the housekeeper assured her. "I can't say whether or not a woman has ever come over for a night, that part isn't my business, but there has never been a woman here for anything more."

That kind of blew Rayne away. A man like Walt would obviously have opportunities to have women live with him, but it seemed he never had. That made Rayne feel even more special.

"Now, have you anything to add to my grocery shopping?" Mrs. Steele asked.

"I can't really think of anything. My friend Sunni wants me to make sure that there is a lot of chocolate in the house for when she visits. But I don't really know what you buy on a regular basis, so I am not sure what to add."

"How about you tell me any foods you absolutely can't stand and things like type of foods you really enjoy rather than specific foods if you can't think of any. That will give me some ideas. But don't be afraid to leave a note on that notebook right there if you ever do think of anything you have a craving for or something you just want to try."

Rayne thought for a minute. "Well, I can't stand peas, bad experience as a child and I just can't go there since then. I'm not big on fresh tomato. I am fine with tomato sauce, salsa, or things like that, but I don't like tomato in a salad or on a burger or whatever." The housekeeper nodded so Rayne continued. "I love Mexican food, Italian food, and the basic plain old standard stuff. I grew up on meat loaf and mac and cheese, simple things, so those are great too."

"Got it," Mrs. Steele assured her. "Now, you finish your breakfast and I will get to work. Let me know if you need anything."

Rayne almost asked if she would help move Rayne's things upstairs, but that seemed a little bit of TMI. The housekeeper probably would figure out that Rayne was sleeping upstairs when her bed was never unmade, but she didn't have to broadcast it.

She finished her breakfast and put her things in the sink since the dishwasher was full of clean dishes from the day before. She thought about putting them away, but she was too excited to begin the search for what kind of car she wanted to buy. And besides, the housekeeper was used to doing it when she was here. Rayne went to the room Walt had told her was his office. She sat in the big comfy office chair and moved the mouse to make the screen come to life. She found the browser icon and clicked on it. *Now, what to put in the search bar*, she wondered to herself. An idea came to mind, so she started typing into the search bar. By the time Walt arrived to pick her up, she had done all her research and knew exactly what she wanted to find.

Chapter Nineteen

Walt pulled into his driveway and realized that Rayne was sitting in one of the chairs on his front porch. An image of her as an old lady and him as an old man sitting in their rocking chairs on the front porch flashed across his brain. It caused two thoughts to come to mind. He really thought that could be his future, but he also knew it was too soon for either of them to be sure that was what they wanted. But he didn't hate the idea of growing old with her.

Rayne stood up when she saw Walt in the driveway. Had he been there long? She had kind of been lost in a daydream. She was thinking about how nice it would be to be sitting here on the front porch with Walt when they were both old and gray. Not that she was ready to start down that road; they still had a lot of getting to know each other territory to go through first. But she had to admit, she didn't hate the idea of growing old with him. She walked toward Walt's car and realized he was looking at her like he wanted to eat her up. She didn't hate that idea either.

When she got into the car, Walt asked if she had narrowed down her car search. She was so excited to tell him that she had. "I want a 2019 Ford Mustang in velocity blue."

"That's pretty specific. You really must have done your research," he commented.

She told him she had. In fact, she was able to tell him of a dealership right here in town that just happened to have one on their lot.

"Well, we'll have lunch in that part of town, and then head over to look at the car," he said. Rayne was so excited about getting a new car that she almost wanted to skip lunch, but she knew that wasn't a good idea, and besides, Walt had spent the whole morning working while she had just been playing on the Internet looking at cars.

Walt took her to a cute little bistro type restaurant in Byron Center.

They shared a delicious meal of soup and sandwiches and some very delicious wine. Walt knew his wine. Rayne never knew what wine to pair with what, but Walt always seemed to get one that blended perfectly.

When they got to the car dealership, Walt cautioned her to not be overzealous. If the salesman got the idea that she had basically already decided to buy a certain car, he wouldn't worry about trying to earn her business or in trying to get her a good deal. If she looked at a few other cars first and then 'just seemed to happen to see another one that she might as well look at it while she was here,' then the salesman might be more likely to try to offer her an upgrade on some aspect rather than just selling her the car as is. That was going to be hard because she did know what she wanted, but she understood the concept of not seeming like she was an easy sell.

They looked at several different cars, sedans, SUVs, even other Mustangs before Rayne looked at the car of her dreams and said, "Oh Walt, look at that one. Isn't that a pretty color of blue?"

Walt never missed a step. As he came to stand beside her, he added, "Yes sweetheart, that's a great color, but I think that price tag was a little more than you were wanting to spend." It wasn't more; obviously, she had millions she could spend, but she caught on to the way Walt was going with this.

"Yes, it is. That color is so pretty, but I'm really not sure I should overspend like that on something that's really not a necessity."

The salesman came right over and started in on his whole sales pitch, telling them all the features she would be getting with that car, how it had absolutely everything she could ever want. It was equipped with all the latest bells and whistles. Rayne had already known all that—she had looked at this very car online—but she still acted like that was good, she liked that, but still, she just wasn't sure she wanted to spend that kind of money. Walt pulled her a little closer to him and gave her a slight squeeze. She was pretty sure he was pleased with her performance.

The salesman asked, "Will you be financing the car? We can get you a great interest rate if your credit is good. You won't be paying a lot in fees and all that, so really it's not all that much more than buying another car at a higher interest rate."

Boy, this guy was really trying to sell this deal. When Walt said, "No, she will be paying cash," the salesman just about blew a gasket.

"Oh, well, um, in that case, let me get my manager. I am sure he can work out a deal that we can all live with." And he disappeared into the dealership.

"You're good at this," Walt complimented her. She thanked him and he gave her a sweet and chaste kiss before a man in a full business suit come out to meet them. This guy looked like a cliché of a car salesman, with a bad haircut and a cheap suit, and it looked like he'd had something with a red sauce for lunch and his attempt to wash it off in the bathroom had only been partially effective. He held out his hand to Walt and introduced himself.

Walt shook his hand but then tilted his head in the direction of Rayne and said, "Nice to meet you, but I'm not the one you have to impress. The lady is buying the car. I'm just here because she needed a ride."

The dealer's face immediately turned red but he turned to Rayne and shook her hand as well. "Now, Mike told me that you are interested in this car, and you want to pay cash, but you think the price is a little out of your budget. Let me say that if you indeed do pay in cash, we have more flexibility with the pricing. If you aren't going to finance it, I can knock two grand off of that sticker price, and I'll even throw in upgraded racing style tires. So, what do you say, ma'am? Can we work out a deal?"

She looked at Walt and she could tell that he was happy with the offer—the look in his eyes just seemed to say it somehow—so she told the dealer, "If you stop calling me ma'am, I am sure we can work something out. Please just call me Rayne. Ma'am makes me think of some old woman." She softened it with what she hoped was a pretty smile and tried show that he hadn't offended her; she just preferred her actual name. They followed him into his office and worked out the rest of the deal. With just a few signatures here and there, Rayne became the proud owner of a Mustang convertible in velocity b. She wasn't sure what all Walt had done to make it so that the car would be available the next day, fancy tires and all, even though she didn't have the money in hand yet. She had left all of that up to him. But whatever he had done, she was so excited to be getting her car so quickly.

When they got home, Walt stopped the car in the driveway in front of the house rather than pulling up to the garage. When Rayne looked at him quizzically, he explained that he needed to swap some things around in the garage and he didn't want the car in the way. He told her to go inside and rest. Even though she was really getting better, thanks to Walt's gentle and sometimes not so gentle nudging, she still did tire more easily than she used to. She knew that was mainly because her body had just spent months doing basically nothing and muscle tone wasn't rebuilt overnight. She went into the house and lay on the bed in the guest room.

She must have dozed off because she woke up to Walt yelling her name from the bottom of the stairs. "I'm in here," she said.

When Walt walked in, he looked a little confused as to why she was in this room instead of his room upstairs. She had to explain quickly; she didn't want him to think that she wasn't ready to move into his room. "I came in here because you were right, I really wore myself out a little today, although it's one of the best ways I can imagine if I am going to overdo it. And because I was hoping that maybe we could move my toiletries and maybe some of my clothes upstairs." She didn't want him to feel like he had to give up all his personal space, so she quickly continued, "We don't have to move everything. I don't want to crowd you out of your own space, just maybe a few things so that I don't have to come down here to brush my teeth every night or to have something to wear while walking through the house."

"You could walk around the house naked," Walt said with an almost evil glint in his eye.

"I don't think I want Mrs. Steele to freak out when a naked woman comes walking down the stairs," Rayne added.

"Well, yes, seeing you walking around naked might be a surprise to her, but I am sure she wouldn't embarrass you about it," Walt assured her. "However, I am very happy to help you move things upstairs to my room. I definitely want you sleeping in there."

Rayne almost asked about the fact that Mrs. Steele had said that he hadn't ever had women around, but she thought that subject was best left untouched. She wasn't sure she ever wanted to know about his past and other women. She knew they existed, but she didn't want to know details.

"I'll tell you what, why don't you go grab what things you need out of the bathroom and take them upstairs? You can stay up there and I will bring your other things and we can figure out where things are going to be put."

Rayne got all her toiletries and what little makeup she had and headed up the stairs. She went into the bathroom and pulled open one of the drawers in the cabinet. It was full of masculine things, so she pulled open the next drawer down. It was full too. She had just about resolved herself to the fact that her things would need to be kept in a case of some sort when she heard Walt say, "Look on the right side."

He was standing at the door watching her. She opened the top drawer on the right, and it was totally empty. She opened the next drawer down and it too was empty. She looked at Walt and he shrugged and nonchalantly said, "I figured I would be sharing the space with a woman someday. It just seemed prudent to start off on a good foot and only use the drawers on one side and save the others for the woman in my life when I found one."

Rayne couldn't help but smile up at him with appreciation. He really had been waiting for someone to come and help fill his life, and apparently the drawers in his bathroom too.

By the time Rayne finished organizing her things into the drawers the way she wanted them, she had heard Walt come and go from the bedroom. She hoped he didn't feel like he needed to empty out closet space for her. She would be fine with just having the basics up here; she could go downstairs when she needed to get dressed to go out or whatever. She walked out of the bathroom to see absolutely every article of clothing she owned, including her bras and underwear, in piles on the massive bed. She shouldn't be embarrassed when she thought of Walt bringing those things up, but she kind of was. Not because he shouldn't see her underthings—he had seen her totally naked for goodness' sake—but she was embarrassed because her things were plain and "functional," not pretty or sexy. When she had been dancing, it was imperative that everything stayed in place, so her choice of undergarments had always reflected that. Maybe that was something else she could buy with her money. Not that she wanted to be a spendthrift, but a few nice things wouldn't hurt, and then she would figure out a charity or a cause that she might be able to help support.

"You didn't have to bring it all up here. I don't want to push you out of your space. I am fine with just one drawer so I can keep the basics up here, or I would be glad to use a closet in another room if that is easier than taking them all back downstairs again," she protested.

"Obviously, you didn't snoop at all while you were here alone this morning." He wiggled his eyebrows up and down. "Look behind that door, sweetheart." He pointed to the door that she had seen him coming out of earlier that day. She walked in and holy crap, this was a walk-in closet that was probably bigger than her entire bedroom back at her apartment. And, just like all the cabinet drawers, the rods and drawers on one entire side were bare and seemed untouched.

She walked back out into the bedroom and smiled. "You really were waiting for a woman," she said.

Walt took her in his arms and said, "No, sweetheart, I wasn't waiting for a woman. I was waiting for you."

Rayne's eyes were starting to water. This guy really knew how to make her feel special. The way he was holding her, she was facing toward the bed. That was when she noticed that he had even brought the pictures of her parents that she had kept on her nightstand downstairs and placed them the same way she had had them on the nightstand on the side of the bed she had slept on last night. Walt was a keeper, as her mom used to say about her dad.

She started organizing all her things into drawers and shelves and the hanging rods in the closet. It didn't really take very long because she didn't have much. She had been living on a tight budget. She had had a part-time job because she wanted to focus mainly on her dancing. Of course, that job had been gone since she was hospitalized so long.

She knew she didn't have to look for a job. If she did things right, her settlement, even after the law firm got paid, could easily support her for the rest of her life. Especially if she made some financially sound investments. She was still lost in her thoughts of what life might be like in the future. She knew she would want to do something—she wasn't just going to sit around and live off the settlement—but she wasn't sure just what she would do yet.

When Walt came to check on her a little later, she told him that there was only one thing she regretted about moving upstairs. When he raised an eyebrow, wondering what she was talking about, she told him, "That room downstairs was made for me. I know you did that because Sunni told you that I love rainbows. And you did an amazing job of it. But now it will be a guest room again and while I am sure that guests will find it beautiful, I'll miss being in there at times."

"Well, then, I have the perfect idea. Why don't we convert that room into a space for you, a 'sitting room' of sorts? If you want some quiet time, or you want to read or plan, you can go sit in the big comfortable chair in there and be surrounded by your rainbows. We can take out the bed and put in a desk or a sofa or whatever you want to have in your room. It can be a study or an office, or whatever you want it to be. We can move the guest room to one of the other rooms up here. That room was set up and decorated with you in mind, so it really should be your room. With it being right off the kitchen, it's a great place for you to relax with a cup of tea or visit with a friend. Not that you aren't welcome to use the living room for company, but if you and Sunni want some privacy to talk or whatever, it's great place for you two to go," Walt suggested.

Rayne threw her arms around him, "That's such a sweet idea. Are you sure you want the guest room to be upstairs, though? You don't want a place for guests on the first floor?"

"Rayne, let me tell you how many 'guests' I have had stay here," Walt began. "Pete stayed here once, when he was a little too drunk to drive home. He slept on the couch. Zak stayed here once because they were painting his apartment and he couldn't stand the fumes. He slept in another bedroom up here. And I've had a gorgeous woman stay with me for a few weeks. She's the only one that ever actually used that as a guest room. I don't really have many guests."

At first Rayne felt a brief pang of jealousy that some other woman had stayed in that room. Maybe she didn't want it to become her sitting room. But then she had a feeling that she was taking this wrong. "You mean me, don't you?" she asked.

"Yep, you would be the only gorgeous woman that has ever stayed in my home." Walt kissed the tip of her nose and then he kissed her on the lips. It was a good thing that her clothes and things were off the bed because he had plans for that space. He walked her back to the edge of the bed while kissing her and began to heat things up.

Chapter Twenty

Three days after Rayne had officially moved into Walt's room, she got a rather cryptic text from him. He asked her to meet him at two this afternoon and he gave her an address. She had replied that she would, but she was going nuts trying to figure out what was going on. Maybe it was a new restaurant he wanted to try, although two was an odd time for lunch or dinner. But she also knew that it was very possible that he had been tied up in court or some such thing and that was going to be the soonest he could get away. Whatever the reason, she would be there, because she really wanted to be anywhere Walt was.

Over the course of the last few days, they had made love in several places, including the hood of her new Mustang. Which by the way, was parked in the garage in the stall closest to the house. Walt had insisted she have the close space, and he had moved his SUV and car over one space in the three-stall garage. They had tried some very interesting and fun things both in and out of the bedroom, like being tied to the headboard with some very soft rope. They had made love on the big table in his formal dining room, in the hot tub, and pretty much any other flat surface. She was getting very addicted to this man and the wonderful things his body could do to her body.

At ten minutes before two she pulled up in front of what looked like an abandoned office building. It was in a nice part of town, not the richy rich part, but one where you also didn't have to worry that your tires might be gone when you came back out. She couldn't understand why Walt would ask her to come here. She looked at the text message again and double checked the GPS in her car, and it confirmed that she was at the right address.

As she got out of the car, Walt was stepping out of the building to come and greet her. When she got to him, he put his arms around her and gave her one of his amazing toe-curling kisses. When they broke apart, he walked over and opened the door for her. She stepped into what had most likely been a reception area at one time, although it was now deserted. There was a counter that she could picture a person sitting behind welcoming any guest who stepped into the room. Walt took her elbow and led her through another door into what looked like a pretty open space, Rayne had no doubt that at one time this room had held numerous cubicles where the "worker bees" sat doing whatever it was that had happened here. She looked around and she could see doors leading off to what were most likely offices and conference rooms.

She looked at Walt, totally puzzled as to what she was doing here. Before she could ask him, a tall thin woman in a very nice business suit came out of one of the rooms. She walked over to Rayne and introduced herself as Susan Miller. She told Rayne how glad she was to meet her and asked her what she thought of the place. Rayne wasn't exactly sure what to say, because she didn't know what she was supposed to be analyzing about the building. Fortunately, Walt spoke up and said, "She isn't sure why she is here, Susan. I kind of set this all up on my own." Susan said something about 'giving them a minute' and walked away. Rayne turned and looked at Walt, very confused.

Walt put up both hands in a sign of surrender. "Just hear me out on this, please sweetheart." She nodded, agreeing that she wouldn't say anything until he had a chance to explain just what was going on. "So I had this idea, and I don't think it's off base. If you look around this space through different eyes, maybe you will see what I'm thinking. Instead of this ratty carpet, I see a polished wooden floor. Instead of that plain gray wall, I see a wall of mirrors." He took her hand and pulled her toward one of the doors. He turned on the light in that room and it had obviously been a large conference room at one point. Walt continued, "Instead of a conference room, I see a room for a smaller group or for one-on-one instruction."

"You see this as a dance studio?" she questioned. Then she had to agree. "I can see what you're saying but why are you asking me about this, Walt? I don't see your point."

Again, he kind of held up his hands in surrender and said, "Sweetheart, there is an old saying that those that can do, and those that can't teach. And you can dance, maybe not to the standard that you used to, but you dance with me almost every day. You are getting stronger, and you wouldn't have to be the only instructor. You can hire people. But I think you alone could make a difference in some little girl's life."

"He's right, you know," Sunni said, walking into the room. Where had she come from? "Listen, Rayne, you have been talking about what you can do with your money. I think Walt has the best idea possible. Open a dance studio, make the tuition affordable. Or make it on a sliding scale or whatever, but you have a gift when it comes to dancing, and maybe you can't make the jumps that you used to or whatever, but you can teach other girls how and maybe you can make some little girl's dream come true."

Rayne had tears in her eyes. Could she really do this? She didn't think so, but the two people she loved most in the world really wanted her to try. "I don't know the first thing about running a dance studio. Even if I could handle the dance instruction or hire other instructors, I wouldn't have a clue how to go about running a business," Rayne protested.

"Jase, get in here," Walt hollered out the door. And a few moments later in walked Jason, Walt's friend and business partner. "Despite the fact that he comes off as a menial bartender most of the time, Jason has one of the best business heads I know. Our brewery would have tanked before we even got it off the ground if it hadn't been for him. I don't like to say too much, because his head is already bigger than the state of Texas, but he really would be a great person to help you with the business side of it all."

He really was pulling out the big guns on this. He'd obviously put some thought into it.

"I don't know, I mean....I... I just don't know." Rayne started pacing.

"Then let us help you. We're here to brainstorm or bounce ideas off of and we will all be behind you 100 percent," Sunni assured her. "I know you can do this, Rayne. Mrs. Boullard is really the only major dance studio in town. She is way on the other side of the city, and the woman has to be in her seventies by now."

Rayne wasn't sure that age was accurate, but she was getting up there in years and the rumor was that none of her kids wanted to keep the dance school open if she ever passed and they took ownership of the building.

"Okay, I'll at least look at the rest of the building and see what I think. I'll keep an open mind," Rayne conceded.

They stepped out of the conference room and Susan was standing there politely waiting to see if they needed anything from her. Walt told her that Rayne would like to see the rest of the building before she made any decisions. Susan showed her the features of each of the floors. There were three, each with a wide-open space covering most of the floor with offices and conference rooms lining two of the walls. One wall was end to end windows and the remaining wall was just a blank space.

Rayne could see how this could make a wonderful dance space. She could see the second and third floors being the main classrooms. The large spaces for classes that had a higher attendance, and the conference rooms for smaller classes. There were adequate bathroom spaces, and some of the offices could easily be made into changing rooms. But she just wasn't sure she had it in her to be a dance instructor.

Sunni walked up to her and Jason and Walt stepped back. Sunni leaned her head against Rayne's forehead and said softly, "Look, hun, I know that this won't be easy, and I know you don't think you have it in you to teach, but think about all those little girls. The ones who have what it takes, and the ones that don't. You can nurture all of them into being the best they can be. I think your dad would be really proud of you, you know. First, you literally made it into the New York Ballet, but then that got taken from you. You have the gift, Rayne, you have the talent. Don't let your injury take that all away from you. Do this for those little girls, do this for your dad, do it for me, but mostly, do it for yourself. You have to believe in something, believe in this. You know I have your back, and you know Walt does too. I don't know Jason super well, but if Walt says he has a great business head, then I am sure he does."

Rayne thought about it for a while. She walked over to the wall of windows and looked out into the bright sunny afternoon. She saw what looked like a park on the opposite corner. She saw a little girl there, and her father was swinging her around. For a minute, Rayne saw herself and her own father in that playful pose. She looked up to the sky and said softly, "Should I do this, Daddy? I wish you were here to help me make this decision." She looked back down, and the little girl was twirling like a ballerina and her father was smiling and clapping for her dance. Rayne figured that was about the best sign her father could give her. She was going to do this.

Epilogue

Three months later

The studio had been filled all day with parents and children stopping by for the open house. Rayne's dance studio was set to open the following week. People had taken tours; some had signed up for classes and some just took the information packet home. Rayne had hired a couple of instructors and she was ready to go. At least as much as she could be. She looked up and closed her eyes and smiled. "This is for you, Daddy," she said softly.

Sunni came to her and they were chatting about the great turnout and how many people had seemed interested. Rayne was dying to ask Sunni about her and Jason and now seemed like the perfect time.

"So what's going on with you and Jason?"

"I don't really know," Sunni said, shaking her head. "I mean, I really like him, and it always seems like he really likes me. But beyond a lot of flirting and a few mostly platonic dates, it doesn't seem like he is looking for anything steady. If you know what I mean."

"Yeah, I kind of thought that was what was going on. He is always flirting with you, and he keeps looking at you when you are in the same room, but he doesn't really want to seem too much like a 'couple,'" Rayne agreed.

"Oh well, I probably don't have time for a relationship anyway. I have my clients and now, my bestie is starting a new business that I will totally support in any way I can." She said it with a smile, but Rayne could tell that her friend would like to have more with the man than he seemed willing to give.

After the guests had all left and it was just down to "friends and family," Walt locked the front door and turned to the remaining people.

"Now the party really starts!" He pointed to where his friend Pete was manning the sound system. he hit a few buttons and some dance music started to play. The people began pairing up to dance to the upbeat song. Everyone seemed to be having fun, and the case of champagne that Walt had bought to celebrate the grand opening was being enjoyed.

He walked over to Rayne and Sunni. "Excuse me, Sunni, but I think this beautiful lady owes me a dance or two," Walt said, reaching for Rayne's hand. They moved out onto the dance floor and danced until the upbeat song was over. Walt immediately pulled Rayne closer as the next song began. It was a slower song, probably a ballad or something like that, but Walt had obviously known that the music was going to change tempo, or maybe he just wanted to hold her closer no matter what the tempo was. She wouldn't complain about that.

She started listening to the words of the song. The singer was talking about remembering their first dance. It was obviously a song that both she and Walt could probably relate to. She would never forget that first time he had taken her out on the dance floor and had supported her so that she could enjoy dancing again.

When the song got to the chorus part, Walt pulled away. The singer was singing, but all she could hear was Walt as he got down on one knee and asked her to be his partner for the rest of his life. He pulled a velvet box out of his pocket as the song went on talking about two people dancing together forever. He opened the box and the most beautiful diamond was staring up at her. She could see the rainbows that the cut of the diamond was making in the light. She couldn't say anything, since tears were streaming down her face; she could only nod her agreement.

Walt stood back up and held the ring out to her. "I had it engraved." She looked at the ring, but the lights had been dimmed slightly so she couldn't really read the letters. She was squinting to try to read it when Walt took it back from her and started to put in on her finger.

"It says, *You're my pot of gold*. I know it's small writing, but it was something I feel every day since I met you." When he had it fully on her hand, she jumped up and wrapped her arms around his neck. "That's a yes, right?" he asked with a devilish grin. "You kind of nodded, but you didn't really say it, so I want to be sure."

"Yes, yes, a thousand times yes," Rayne said before going in for a kiss. When they broke the kiss, she realized that everyone was staring at them. Walt turned so they were facing their other guests and announced, "She said yes!" even though most of them probably already knew that. Everyone lifted their glass of champagne and toasted the start of the rest of their lives.

The End

Author's Note

I began this book in November 2018. In December of 2018, real life hit my family pretty hard with medical issues. Of course, writing got set on the back burner. I was finally able to finish it this last November. As a side note to that, if you have ever wanted to give writing a try, I highly recommend NaNoWriMo- it's a great time to challenge yourself to at least get a good start on your manuscript. You never know what you can start with 60,000 words.

This book has been a joy but also a learning experience for me. I hope you fall in love with Walt and Rayne and all their friends as much as I have.

An excerpt from Opaque Skye

(Five Sloths Brewing Book 2)

Coming April 2020

Zak sat drumming his thumbs on the steering wheel and glancing around while waiting for whatever it was that had traffic at a standstill at 8:50 a.m. on this sunny Monday morning. He was going to be late for work, as usual. Not that it mattered. When you were the son of a senior managing partner at the law firm, no one really had the balls to say anything about you strolling into the office at 9:15 or even 9:30, for that matter. Although lately, his parents had both been getting on to him about being more responsible, taking some initiative, maybe even settling down a little from his playboy ways. But, at 27, who wanted to settle down? Even though his life had been what some would call "charmed," he still had some living he wanted to do.

Sure, he had all the best things in life growing up. Sure, he had gotten into all the best schools because of his last name and his father's status as an alumnus. That didn't mean that he hadn't earned his good grades. He had studied hard to graduate at the top of his class in both high school and college. His grades at Harvard Law School had proven that he did what it took to get the job done. But, now that was over and he had passed the bar exam, it was time to live a little.

Zak's eyes caught on a woman getting out of an SUV parked alongside the road. Man, she was hot. Her long amber hair was not curly, but not really straight either. It framed a beautiful face. High cheekbones, gorgeous lips, and those eyes. He couldn't tell exactly what color they were from this distance, but definitely something light, like blue or maybe gray. Either way, they looked like eyes a man like him could get lost in while he sank deep into her body as it writhed in pleasure under him. A body which, from what he could see, was built for pleasure. She wasn't pencil thin like so many of the women who came on to him in the clubs. She wasn't fat by any means either, but she did have just enough curves that a man could get lost for hours exploring them.

Triskelion

A spin-off from Five Sloths Brewing

Coming Fall 2020

Brett...big brother...first to become a Green Beret… first to serve his country, first to protect his siblings…. first to step up and make a place for his brothers to come home to.

Trevor… middle kid…. wasn't the oldest, wasn't the youngest, so he became determined to be the smartest. When he joined the Green Berets, it was because the Marines would rather he was hacking for them than into them.

Riley… little brother...baby of the family. When your only family is already Green Beret, what else are you going to be? Sometimes he wishes he had died with his squad….sometimes he's glad he didn't, but all the time, he wishes he could really walk away… not from life, not from reality, not from the only blood he's got left… but from the pain and the memories… yeah, those he wishes he could walk away from.

Triskelion is a series about Brett, Trevor and Riley Dawson. Three brothers, all former Green Beret.

Triskelion Motorcycles, their bike shop is their 'every day' job. It's also the location for the offices of their bodyguard and private investigating services for people that need their skills.

Triskelion turns the heat up a few notches from my Five Sloths Brewing series.

About Robin Andrews

Robin Andrews still lives in the same small town that she grew up in. She began college headed for a legal career. While she still went into the legal arena, she set aside the idea of becoming an attorney for the much more rewarding life of a mother and grandmother. She has been married for thirty-five years. She lives with her husband and her miniature Labradoodle, Hope.

She is the mother to three adult children (two boys, one girl) and grandmother to three grandchildren (two girls, one boy). She loves taking her family to the local fitness center for family swim days.

Her greatest joys in life are writing, reading and spending time cuddling with her grandkids.

Website: www.ste-entertainment.com

I would love to have you join my readers group on Facebook: Robin's Readers Nest.
https://www.facebook.com/groups/898899640504649/?ref=share

Other books by Robin Andrews

Opaque Skye Five Sloths Brewing Book 2
Coming April 2020

Encouraging Autumn Five Sloths Brewing Book 3

Resistant Summer Five Sloths Brewing Book 4

Embracing Sunni Five Sloths Brewing Book 5

www.ingramcontent.com/pod-product-compliance
Lightning Source LLC
Chambersburg PA
CBHW051951170626
46808CB00007B/2571